Please return or renew this item  **East Sussex**
by the last date shown. You may **County Council**
return items to any East Sussex
Library. You may renew books
by telephone or the internet.

0345 60 80 195 for renewals

0345 60 80 196 for enquiries

Library and Information Services
eastsussex.gov.uk/libraries

04578882

MAL PEET

MR GODLEY'S PHANTOM

David Fickling Books

Mr Godley's Phantom
is a
DAVID FICKLING BOOK

First published in Great Britain by
David Fickling Books,
31 Beaumont Street,
Oxford, OX1 2NP

www.davidficklingbooks.com

Hardback edition published 2018
This edition published 2019

Text © Mal Peet

Illustrations © Ian Beck

Mal Peet Tribute © Daniel Hahn

978-1-910989-52-4

1 3 5 7 9 10 8 6 4 2

Papers used by David Fickling Books are from well-managed forests and other respon-
sible sources.

DAVID FICKLING BOOKS Reg. No. 8340307

A CIP catalogue record for this book is available from the British Library.

Typeset in 11½/15¾ pt Sabon by Falcon Oast Graphic Art Ltd.
Printed and bound in Great Britain by Clays Ltd, Elcograf S.p.A.

Reprinted by permission of Harvard University Press: THE POEMS OF
EMILY DICKINSON, edited by Thomas H. Johnson, Cambridge, Mass.:
The Belknap Press of Harvard University Press, Copyright © 1951, 1955 by the
President and Fellows of Harvard College. Copyright © renewed 1979, 1983
by the President and Fellows of Harvard College. Copyright © 1914, 1918,
1919, 1924, 1929, 1930, 1932, 1935, 1937, 1942, by Martha Dickinson
Bianchi. Copyright © 1952, 1957, 1958, 1963, 1965, by Mary L. Hampson.

Long Years apart – can make no
Breach a second cannot fill –
The absence of the Witch does not
Invalidate the spell –

The embers of a Thousand Years
Uncovered by the Hand
That fondled them when they were Fire
Will stir and understand –

Emily Dickinson

PART ONE

An Infection of Evil

1945–1947

1

AFTER THE WAR, after he was out, Martin Heath did almost nothing for several months. He was still young but his dreams – nocturnal and diurnal – belonged to an older man, a man much damaged and long steeped in blood. Death operated the film projector inside his head.

He could not imagine returning to Cambridge and told himself he was too busy being haunted to get a job. To hold one down. He took himself to the doctor. Old McInnis, his father's partner, whose cold hands had probed his childhood, had retired. The new doctor was a woman. He had never entertained the notion of such a thing. He'd intended to exaggerate his symptoms: the tremor, the headaches. To his very great surprise he found himself bent in the chair, weeping, leaking sobs and snot. She wrote out a prescription and a letter declaring him unfit for work on medical grounds. She also offered to refer him to a psychiatrist: an offer he declined, silently offended, not considering himself mad in any way. Thereafter he went, on Tuesdays, to the Labour Exchange to collect his dole, although sometimes he forgot.

He spent two days getting his father's car operational. The Riley had grieved, dulling, in the garage for over a year. His mother had no use for it – she'd never learned to drive – but had been unable to bring herself to sell it. Her husband had died behind its wheel, after all. Parked, smoking his pipe, watching girls leave the High School. Cardiac arrest. The hot spillage from his pipe had left a scorch on his flies.

Martin had been in Italy when the news reached him. The balls-up they were now calling the Battle of Anzio. A lull in the German shelling. It had taken him three attempts to understand the letter; it was as if the overhead roar of American planes had made him temporarily illiterate. The army chaplain was a Canadian. One of his eyes was hidden under the bulge of a field-dressing, the other blinked incessantly.

The car's upholstery still smelled of Dad: tobacco, the almondy whiff of Brylcreem, leather polish. There were two hoarded jerry cans of petrol in a corner of the garage. Martin got the car started with the crank handle and nursed it to Jessop's.

The mechanic who came out of the workshop onto the forecourt and greeted him by name was Jessop's son. What was his first name? Shit, it had gone. Fallen into one of those gaps, fissures, in his head.

'Wotcha, Martin. Heard you was home. How's tricks?'

They'd been at school together. Jessop the Younger still looked like a schoolboy: the same girlish fringe of biscuit-coloured hair, the same circular, thick-lensed specs behind which his eyes floated, blue tadpoles in a jar.

'Yeah. All right. You know.'

'Still the same ole place. Nothin's changed. You've not missed much.'

He could think of nothing acceptable to say. The honest words hung silent in the air between them:

I can't talk to you. I've been away in a war. You haven't.

And: *It wasn't my fault. I would've gone. It was my eyesight.*

'I'm sorry about your ole man, Martin. It don't seem fair.'

'Yeah, well. Anyway . . .'

Jessop's eyes swam over to the car. 'But you got the old Riley goin.'

'Only just. It needs work. Clutch cable. Distributor . . .'

Jessop held up a hand, the oily palm like an etching.

'Don't you worry. You come back next week, I'll have her running like a dream. Long as she don't need parts. We can't get parts for love nor money these days. Shall we say Tuesday?'

As they were parting Jessop called, 'Some of us get together down the Plough, Fridays. You might wanner drop by, you fancy a jar.'

Martin saluted vaguely. 'Yeah,' he lied, 'I might do that.'

He got himself a petrol ration book and made occasional trips, usually aimless, often to the coast. He'd park the car and sit for unmeasured periods of time willing the clouds to remain clouds, not smoke. Willing the Devil's projector to shut down.

On one occasion, near Lulworth, the desire to drive off the cliff was very strong. He was about to release the handbrake when sudden rain squalled against the windscreen, and for some reason this changed his mind. He drove to a pub where he drank, shakily, a half of bitter and a whisky. The only other customers were two elderly men who watched him sidelong and suspiciously.

He could scarcely remember being the boy in whose room he slept, although its contents had a disturbing familiarity. The jigsaw puzzles in their boxes: *2 pieces missing, sky* in fastidious writing. The Sherlock Holmes adventures. John Buchan. *This book belongs to M J Heath.* The biscuit tin containing sets of cigarette cards held together by rubber bands, now dry and perished. Cricketers, film stars. Regimental uniforms.

He'd awake, gasping, into the dark no-man's-land between Then and Now.

He drank, at first to keep his mother company. They often played cards in the evenings. Some games necessitated a dummy hand, which his mother dealt to the place at the table where her husband no longer sat, as if he'd merely left the room to visit the lavatory. They played with the wireless on, not listening to it but using it as a reason not to talk. She drank gin, topping up her glass in the kitchen between games. As the evening wore on, mistakes would enter her play and, eventually, she would become tearful.

'I don't know who you are any more, Martin.'

Or: 'I lost your father, and now I feel as though I've lost you.'

Or: 'I feel doubly bereaved.'

So Martin started to work his way through his father's Scotch while they played. It helped him murmur the slurred phrases that seemed appropriate or required. Combined with the tranquillisers from the new doctor, it sometimes unmonstered his sleep.

He never went to the Plough, but when he felt he should try human society he went to the Lion and Lamb on the other side of town where he was less well known. For a while he was content to eavesdrop, timing his pints, sitting at the bar like someone perfectly happy in his solitude; a man spending an hour or two away from his wife, perhaps. Then one night he got into a fight. Some buffoon said something about Hitler having the right idea about the Jews, say what you like. His mates laughed, agreeing. Martin put his drink down carefully on the beer mat, stood up and took the man by the throat. By the time he stumbled out into the street a mere three minutes later he'd damaged the man and two others.

Because he'd known how to, because it was uncomplicated.

Because he felt released by it.

He walked a hundred yards or so, no one following him, until he came to a stone horse trough. He sat on its rim and lit a cigarette. When he took it from his mouth it had blood on it. He waited until he heard the police car, then stood up and stepped into the road where he would be clearly illuminated by its headlamps.

The sergeant knew him, had always known him, and had read of Corporal Heath's gallantry, his honours, in the local press. He brought Martin a cup of tea and left him sitting in a small cubicle next to the Duty Desk.

When he came back he said, 'I've had a word, Martin, and we won't be taking this any further. There was provocation, the way we see it.'

'Thanks.'

'I know what you've been through. Well, I don't, but I can imagine. But let's have no more of this, there's a good lad. Think of your mother.'

Her forty-eighth birthday fell in November. Martin drove her to Dorchester through filthy weather and treated her to afternoon tea at the Royal Wessex Hotel. He slipped the waiter a shilling to seat them closer to the fire. For the first time since his return she wore make-up, and nothing black. She handed her coat – lavender tweed with a fur-trimmed collar – to the waiter and then, walking to their table, glanced at herself in a tall wall-mounted mirror and touched up her hair.

During the meal Martin noticed that two well-dressed middle-aged men at a nearby table glanced at her a number of times; he saw one of them purse his lips and nod appreciatively at his companion. It seemed to Martin – a slight adjustment of her posture, a half-smile not occasioned by the slice of ersatz Dundee cake in front of her – that his mother was aware of this apparent admiration. And with a shock that was almost physical – he shifted in his chair as if to counteract it – he realised that his mother was still an attractive woman, one who might not be content to remain a widow. He suffered a brief, grotesque vision of her in a hotel bedroom with one of the sleek businessmen. His cup shook; he had to use both hands to lower it onto the saucer. Yes. His mother might well be ready for a new life.

One without him in it. One for which he was, in

fact, an obstacle.

He wrote to his tutor at Trinity. It took him a while to remember the man's name.

The reply was prompt and cordial. Yes, in the circumstances, Martin could resume his degree at the beginning of the Lent term which, Doctor Merrett reminded him 'no doubt unnecessarily', commenced on the fifteenth of January.

2

HE LASTED three terms.

Allowances were made for his behaviour. After all, there were a good many ex-servicemen at Cambridge; it was not surprising that a few of them were a little, well, erratic. That chap at Corpus Christi who went to pubs and challenged customers to drink a yard of ale out of his tin leg. The former Bomber Command fellow at Peterhouse, who liked to sing hymns in Coe Fen, naked.

At the beginning of December 1946, lacking a better option, Martin went home to Dorset for the Christmas vacation. At his mother's insistence, which he considered perverse, he accompanied her to a round of dinners, drinks parties and lunches. He was surprised by how many of these there were, by how extensive his mother's acquaintanceships had become. It seemed to him that she might have been more the merry widow without him in tow. Which was, perhaps, why she had him in tow.

Conversations at these tiresome occasions soon became predictable: the reckless socialism of Atlee's Labour government, especially the unworkable idea of a free national health service; rationing, and ways to get round it; the continuing and ridiculous presence of German and Italian prisoners of war in the country and the cost of feeding and housing them.

And how Martin was getting on at Cambridge.

'Margery tells me you're reading History, is that right?'

'Yes.'

'Fascinating subject. Bit of a history buff myself. Any particular, ah, area of interest? I'm rather hot on the Tudors, personally.'

Somehow Martin managed not to say, *I'm specialising in the theory of history as complete balls. That historians are preposterous liars and always have been.*

That theses, overviews, explications, are all self-serving nonsense. That the truth is that history is merely the story of mankind stumbling from one brutish fuck-up to the next. And I know because I was very recently part of one.

Instead, he said, 'I'm rather interested in ninth-century Persia at the moment. Shall I fetch us another drink?'

He couldn't decide whether to return to Trinity or not. Then, in the middle of January, the matter was taken out of his hands.

A raging polar winter did what Hitler had failed to do: it invaded England, crushed it, brought it to a standstill. Snow levelled its contours and imposed a terrible silence. Army troops worked alongside prisoners of war to dig out railway cuttings which, the following day, filled again. Tides froze. Canals solidified. Snowploughs were swallowed by snow. Coal, already rationed, became unobtainable. Electricity was intermittent. Telephone lines collapsed.

Martin and his mother spent most of their days in their beds, nursing warmth. When the electricity did come on, they heated canned foods and ate them hurriedly. Now and again, wearing lots of clothes, they played cards by candlelight. The radio came and went unpredictably. Like everyone else, they presumed this waywardness of the weather would be short-lived.

It was not. Britain's paralysis continued through February. There were rumours of cannibalism in the north of Scotland.

In early March, in a last wild gesture, the winter flung an icy blizzard across the country. The thaw that followed it was accompanied, calamitously, by endless rain. England's rivers overran their courses; half the country was flooded. The East Anglian fens, in which Cambridge sat islanded, became a vast lake.

Martin waited. And continued to wait.

When postal services resumed in April he received a letter. The envelope was of quality paper, not the usual flimsy stuff. Basingstoke postmark. Martin's reluctance to open it irritated his mother.

Late in the morning he took it up to his room.

A cursive letterhead: *Whittier, Locke & Sons, Solicitors & Commissioners of Oaths*. Two pages, typed. He looked at the signature, three verticals and two wriggles of black ink above its translation, James R. Locke, and below that the words *Junior Partner*. It meant nothing to him at first.

```
Dear Martin,
(I almost wrote 'Corp'!)
A little bird (no names no pack drill,
let's call it a Cambridge Warbler) tells
me that you are having some difficulty
in settling back into Civvy Street. I
sympathise. I'm not finding it easy myself.
I work with colleagues, good decent people,
most of them, who haven't the first idea
```

Martin stopped reading, looked again at the signature. His blood thumped inside his ears and it seemed to him that the air in the room had become difficult to breathe. James Locke. 'Lucky' Locke. *Lieutenant* Locke. Lucky and insanely brave. Brave enough to cry in front of his men when they entered Hell at Belsen.

The projector whirred. The images flickered, steadied. He could not stop them. Lucky sobbing obscenities while forcing SS women, his pistol to their heads, to drag bodies to mass graves. The silent skeletons, who yet moved on legs of bone, walking towards him, slow as dreamers but all eyes. The others, heaped, skulls muddled with shin bones, claws, shrunken genitals. Shit and slurry and decomposition. Martin had felt neither rage nor even revulsion. Rather, it was like discovering that he had contracted an incurable disease; that, having inhaled the miasma of death, he could never be well again. That his heart might eat itself.

He dropped the letter and doubled up on the bed, his breathing making phlegmy moans in his throat. After several minutes he sat up and fumbled out the bottle he kept in the drawer with his underwear. He took a slug straight from the neck and let the burn filter down into his chest, then went to the window and shoved it open. The sky was full of ash. No, not ash; snow. Dear God, not again. But the flakes vanished as soon as they touched ground. He lit a cigarette, but its taste was vile and he flicked it out onto the lawn.

After a while he took up the letter again. His eyes skittered along the text. He had to make himself read every sentence at least twice. The lieutenant dwelt awhile on the subject of the recent 'apocalyptic' weather.

```
. . . Anyway, to come to the point: a
position has come up that I thought might
interest you . . . Dear old chap called
Godley, used to be in business with my
grandfather . . . in Devon, a quiet spot . . .
thought a combination of being busy and
solitude might suit you, if you feel anything
like the way I do . . . if you are interested,
call me at the above number and I'll give
you details and wrtite you a reference.
Or if you don't fancy talking, drop me a
line . . . you took bnloody goiod care of
the blokes, Martin. Time to take care of
yourself now
```

He folded the letter back into its envelope, put it into his coat pocket and went for a walk. There was no sign of snow having fallen. He assumed he'd imagined it.

Over dinner, yielding to his mother's curiosity, he said, 'From my old platoon commander.'

'Oh, yes?'

'Yes. One of the good guys.'

She grimaced at the Americanism. Waited.

He said, 'This is real ham, isn't it? Where on earth did you get it?'

For a few days he tried to put the letter out of his mind. Because thinking about the letter meant thinking about Lucky Locke and thinking about the lieutenant meant thinking about all the rest of it. Watching it.

Then, late one morning while he was poking about in the sodden garden, he heard his mother singing, accompanying the wireless. A sentimental love song he half remembered from before the war. Motionless, he listened to her for a minute or so, then dropped the trowel into the flower bed and went inside. He washed his hands then picked up the telephone, dialled 0 and gave the operator the number in Basingstoke.

3

HE WAS ATTRACTED to the place, felt a sort of affinity with it, as soon as he saw it. Burra Hall was, he supposed, a mere hundred years old, if that, but occupied its leafy cleft in the moor as if it had always done so; as if, in fact, it had been formed by the same geological upheaval that had created the rocky hill behind it and the heaped, harsh slabs that capped it. The house was built of that same granite, but its architectural details – window bays, lintels, the two columns that supported the portico – were of a more mellow and paler stone.

Out of habit he worked out a plan of attack on the

place. The Bren gun on that higher ground to the right. Good cover: gorse, jumbled rock. Move the platoon up along the dead ground between the lawn and the paddock. Grenades, then—

He closed his eyes, shook his head. *Stop it.*

To steady himself, he stepped off the drive into the lee of its hedge and lit a cigarette.

He was edgier than he'd hoped he'd be, and tired. The journey had taken him much longer than he'd estimated. Four changes of train. Nothing was on time and no one cared very much. At Exeter, his train had waited for half an hour behind a delayed troop train bound for Plymouth. Its engine hissed steam and huffed smoke up into the station's canopy while grinning, nervous conscripts lugged kitbags up and down the platform in response to contradictory orders yelled at them by exasperated NCOs.

When his own train – a mere two carriages, thinly populated – did eventually leave, it trundled almost immediately into absurdly lovely scenery. Greening willows in water meadows. Bronze cattle in pastures. The low swell of wooded hills. *England's green and pleasant land*, Martin thought. *What I, we, fought for.* He would've liked to have felt some sort of ownership of it and that it, in turn, should somehow acknowledge its debt to him. Just beyond somewhere called Crediton a deer took fright and fled. Bounced. Flashes of white rump.

He'd felt not better, exactly, but certainly more sure of himself, after the train turned west and the harsh flank of Dartmoor rose to the left of the train. He went out into the corridor and unfastened the leather latch of a window. Cool air coiled in. A distant tor reminded him of, took him back to, a wrecked hilltop village in Italy. He took the hip flask from his coat pocket. After a while he went back to his compartment and somehow fell asleep. He awoke when someone shook his shoulder.

'Your stop, young sir,' the conductor said. 'Best be lookin lively.'

Leaving the train, Martin unfolded Godley's letter once again. The handwriting was neat, fastidious and difficult to read:

I extend my apolgies for being unable to arrange for someone to meet you from the train ... thirty minutes brisk walk...

21

the important thing is not to miss the signpost indicating Leeworthy. Burra itself is not signposted.

He'd got lost. There were no signposts. They'd been taken down during the war, and Devon had not considered it a priority to re-erect them. How come bloody Godley didn't know that? He stopped at a cottage where a dog dithered between welcome and attack. The woman was garrulous and almost incomprehensible. Martin had persuaded her to draw a map on the reverse of Godley's letter. It was obvious that she'd never attempted such a thing before. She'd seethed with questions she didn't know how to ask.

Martin ground the cigarette under his foot and looked at his watch. Shit. Almost two hours beyond ETA. Poor show. Bad start. Better, perhaps, to call the whole thing off. Go home, write a letter saying something had cropped up. Except that he couldn't get home, not now.

*

The door had a brass knocker in the shape of a hound's head. He thudded it three times and waited. The door was opened by a young woman dressed in black. Only her pale face and white apron distinguished her from the dimness behind her. Her eyes were drawn to the bag he carried. For lack of anything more suitable, he'd packed his overnight things in his father's medical bag. It seemed to worry her.

'Yes?'

'I'm Martin Heath. I think I'm expected.'

'Oh. Us'd more or less given up on you. Didn think you was comin.'

'Sorry. The trains . . .'

'Yes. You'd best come in, anyhow.'

He stepped into a gloomy hall and waited for his eyes to adjust. The space smelled of aged wealth.

'I'll take your coat. And your bag. This's where they'll be, see?'

'Yes. Thank you.'

'Mr Godley's in the study. He's put off tea, waitin. Foller me.'

She opened a door on the left-hand side of the hall.

'Sir? Mr Heath is here.'

The room seemed both crammed and unoccupied. It was full of ponderous furniture and stale air. A narrow pathway led to a Turkish rug in front of a fireplace in which a fire struggled for life. Two high-backed arm-chairs faced it, angled slightly towards each other. A bony hand emerged from one of these and, using the arm of the chair for leverage, an old man unfolded himself and turned to greet Martin. He was wearing a tartan dressing gown over a white shirt and a black waistcoat and grey herringbone tweed trousers.

'Ah. Mr Heath. I had almost abandoned hope. One has to make allowances, of course, things being what they are. We've won again, but still nothing works, eh?'

'Yes. I'm sorry. It took longer than I'd thought. I'm sorry if I've inconvenienced you.'

'Think nothing of it. Annie, please ask Mrs Maunder to prepare tea, then tell her she is free to go. She'll have made supper, I presume?'

'Yes, sir. A shepherd's pie and cabbage from the garden. I'll pop it in the oven.'

'Excellent. We'll have it at six thirty.'

Martin wanted to turn and look at the girl because she was, perhaps, beautiful, but he could not drag his eyes from Harold Godley because the old man fright-ened and fascinated him. Godley was very elderly and so thin that he hardly occupied his clothes. They were of good quality; nevertheless, he resembled a scarecrow,

24

a mannikin made of sticks and dressed in whatever came to hand. There was room enough between his frail neck and his stiff shirt-collar to insert a pair of hands. His head was a skull dressed in skin and kitted out with a pair of spectacles and a smile stretched over yellow teeth.

'Come and take a seat, Mr Heath. You must be feeling somewhat worn out.'

'No, I'm . . . Yes, thank you.'

Martin made himself walk over to the old man and take his outstretched hand. It closed on his own like the claws of a hermit crab.

'Sit, sit. Now then.'

Martin sat. Godley regarded him intently for a few moments, as if trying to memorise his features then, from somewhere within his clothes, he produced a letter.

'Jim Locke's reference. I have to say I was impressed. Very impressed. He writes that you are, were, ah, "the bravest and most professional soldier he had the honour of serving with". Hmm? The Distinguished Conduct Medal and no fewer than three Mentions in Dispatches. He goes so far as to say that in his opinion, your actions during the Italian campaign merited the Victoria Cross. It seems I find myself in the company of a hero, Mr Heath. Hmm?' Godley looked up, aiming his forced and yellow smile. 'Am I embarrassing you? Yes, I see that I am. I apologise. I have offended against your modesty. You would probably rather not discuss these matters.'

'I left university and joined the army when I was nineteen,' Martin said. 'I've never had a proper job. I'd rather like to know what this one involves. What would be expected of me.'

'Yes, of course. But please indulge an old man's curiosity. You come from a professional background and, as you say, you were at university when war broke out. One would have thought you were officer material. But you chose to stay in the ranks. Hmm?'

Something slightly sharp, even accusatory, had come into the old man's voice. Martin shifted uneasily in the armchair. A perfunctory knock at the door rescued him. The girl, Annie, backed in towing a tea trolley. She parked it in front of the fire and pulled two small tables closer to the chairs.

'Shall I serve, sir?'

Godley leaned back and closed his eyes. 'Yes, Annie. Thank you.'

Tea in good china and scones spread with what looked like real blackcurrant jam. Martin realised he was hungry. The girl was slim but shapely. Furtively, he watched the shifting of her haunches within the black dress as she bent to the tables.

When she'd gone Godley took a small sip of tea and returned his cup to its saucer.

'I – we – need a man about the place. Had one, until a while ago, name of Walters. Perfectly good fellow, but he couldn't stand the solitude. As you have no doubt observed, this is a lonely spot. I am reduced to two staff. Annie' – he gestured toward the door – 'lives in. Cook, Mrs Maunder, lives in the village with her sister, who is an invalid. She makes a decent scone, wouldn't you say, given the austerity of the times? Hmm?'

Martin, his mouth full, nodded.

'I employ a part-time gardener, Mr Gates, but he's getting on in years and finds the heavier work a challenge.'

'I see. So you need someone to help him out?'

Godley did not answer. His gaze had drifted off and his face had slackened into an expression of intolerable grief. Martin felt a familiar squirm of fear, of dread.

'Sir?'

It came out as a whisper. He cleared his throat.

'Sir?'

Godley twitched and came back. 'Hmm?'

'You were saying that Mr Gates could do with some help. In the garden.'

'Yes. If you are so inclined.' Godley cleared his throat. A bulge between sinews. 'The fact is, Mr Heath, that we – that is to say Annie and I and perhaps even the redoubtable Mrs Maunder – feel vulnerable. Isolated. During the war, we felt that we were, as they say, "toughing it out" like everyone else. We felt that we – you'll find this laughable, no doubt – that we were "doing our bit". But now . . .'

Again his gaze wavered. He took another sip of tea. It seemed restorative.

'Are you a good driver, Mr Heath?'

'Er, yes, I think so.'

'Good. Now, if you have finished your tea, be so kind as to press that button beside the mantelpiece.'

Martin did so and heard a bell jangle, distantly. A minute later Annie came into the room.

Godley resurrected himself from his chair. 'Mr Heath and I are going to inspect the vehicles, Annie. While there's still light.'

The girl looked directly at Martin for the first time; a glance that was appraising, perhaps even hostile. 'Yessir. I'll get your things.'

She went out, only to wait in the hallway with the old man's scarf, black homburg hat and cane. Then she led the way to the back door and held it open.

Passing through behind Godley, Martin said, 'Thank you.'

She dipped a little curtsey that seemed to him ironic.

The flagstoned courtyard was by now half-shadowed. Crossing into the light, Godley – in his dressing gown and hat, leaning on his cane, walking as if brittle – might have been an ancient music-hall comedian making his farewell entrance onto the stage.

The yard was entirely enclosed except for a wide entrance at its far end. To the left, a long two-storey building, its dark stonework punctuated by stable doors and small windows under brick arches. At the far end of this structure, a pair of much wider doors; a coach house, Martin supposed. On the right-hand side of the yard, a shorter building of similar design and an ivy-webbed wall with a heavy-looking door set into it.

An easy place to defend, Martin thought, looking around, calculating fields of fire. *Also an easy place to get trapped.*

A sombre little vehicle was parked beside the

entrance to the yard. A bull-nose Morris van painted, or possibly repainted, a dull green.

'The workhorse,' Godley said. 'The runabout. Entirely at your disposal, should you accept the position. Now, what I want to show you is over here.'

The coach-house doors were suspended from small wheels set into an overhead iron runner. At Godley's instruction Martin hauled on the left-hand one. It squealed resistance.

'Could use a spot of grease, I'd say, sir.'

'Yes, yes, I dare say.'

Impatience in the old man's voice. Martin shouldered the door open to its full extent and turned. Then paused because something large and gleaming had caught the light. Columns topped by a triangular cornice supporting a winged goddess. The silver frontage of a Roman temple with enormous glass eyes.

'The other door, if you please, Mr Heath.'

Martin groaned the other door aside. Then, without waiting to be invited, stepped into the coach house and fell in love.

'Jesus.'

Behind him, Godley chuckled; four dry, chickeny sounds.

'Indeed, Mr Heath.'

'A Rolls.'

'Yes. A Rolls-Royce Phantom Three Sedanca de Ville, to be precise.'

'It's . . . huge. Beautiful. My God.'

'Feel free to inspect her, Mr Heath.'

Martin walked the length of the car. *Christ*, he thought, *must be eighteen feet if it's an inch.* And as tall as himself. *Must weigh three tons, at a guess.* Its bonnet and bodywork pale, off-white. *Ivory*, that would be it. Roof, wings, running boards black. The rear of the machine a voluptuous concave curve. He felt a shameful desire to press himself into it. He peered into the passenger compartment, which seemed to be upholstered in the same ivory-coloured leather and contained inscrutable items of inbuilt, wood-veneeered furniture. It was separated from the driver's narrow accommodation by a glass screen. The dashboard was an array of switches and instrumentation that would have seemed more at home in the cockpit of a bomber. He felt a fearful craving to climb into her, explore her, start her up.

He returned to the front of the machine and put his hand on the mascot perched, leaning forward, above the radiator grille. Not a goddess, and not wings. A thrilled and human young woman in a flimsy night-gown giving herself to the wind. With nice breasts.

'The Spirit of Ecstasy, Mr Heath. Allegedly modelled on the mistress of Lord Beaulieu. She's sometimes, rather vulgarly, referred to as Emily. Now then, let us return to the house. I'm feeling a little cold. You'd be welcome to have another look at the car in the morning before you leave.'

'Yes. Thank you. I'd like to do that.'

Martin took a parting look at the Rolls. In the black billow of her wing he caught a glimpse of himself, comically warped and elongated.

He heaved the doors shut. Godley took his arm in a claw.

4

MARTIN LEANED AGAINST the kitchen dresser smoking a cigarette and watching Annie prepare her employer's supper tray. Silver knife and fork and a rolled napkin in a silver ring. A glass of water and a smaller glass containing a brownish solution. Two white pills in a tiny white dish. (*Take mine*, he reminded himself.) A side plate onto which she served a child's helping of shepherd's pie and cabbage.

'He allers eat in the dinin room,' Annie said, unasked, 'though tis cold as hell most the year. But he has his standards, see?'

She tidied her hair and lifted the tray.

'We'll eat in here.'

While she was gone, Martin took a nip from his hip flask.

They sat at opposite ends of the kitchen table. Annie ate quickly, keeping her eyes on the task. Martin had never eaten a meal alone with a woman other than his mother. It was interesting that Annie's hair was disobedient and that he could not tell how old she was. Younger than himself, probably. She was, he thought, very attractive, although it was difficult to judge the attractiveness of a woman eating cabbage. She caught him looking at her.

'D'you drink?'

'Pardon?'

'D'you like a drink?'

'Yes, sometimes.'

She scraped her chair away from the table and opened a cupboard. She came back to the table carrying a bottle of red wine recorked at an angle. She fetched two glasses from the dresser and filled them to the top.

'Cheers,' he said, then, 'Blimey, this is good.' He peered at the label. Fleurie. 'It really is good stuff.'

'Is it? I dunno. There's tons of it downstairs. I just like a drop with me dinner.'

'And why not?' Martin heard a jollier version of himself say.

She finished eating before he did and leaned back in her chair. 'So,' she said, 'you gornter take the job?'

'I'm not sure. I don't really know what it entails.'

'Come again?'

'What I'd be supposed to do, exactly. Mr Godley was a bit vague, to be honest.'

'Be here. Be handy about the place. Drive the car. He does love a ride in it now and again.'

'Well, yes. Who wouldn't?'

Annie took a gulp of the Fleurie and smiled at him for the first time. A smile with more than a touch of mockery in it. She had good teeth.

'Took a shine to it, did you? The Roller?'

'It's . . . amazing. Scared me a bit, to tell the truth.' He took out his packet of Players. 'Do you smoke? Would you like one?'

She glanced at the kitchen clock. 'I don't, as a rule. But just this once, then. Ta.'

He lit their cigarettes, then said, 'There was a bloke before, wasn't there? Walters, was it? What was he like?'

She shrugged. 'All right. Oldish. He couldn't stick it, though, out here miles from anywhere. He went a bit doolally towards the end. D'you reckon you could stick it?'

'I don't know. I think so. I think it's a rather beautiful place.'

She grunted. 'It's not so bad now spring's on the way. The winters can be a right bugger. Back in February' – she pronounced it *febbry* – 'we didn' know whether we'd freeze afore we starved or the other way about.'

She exhaled smoke and fanned it away with her hand.

'What's your story, anyhow?'

'Sorry?'

'What were you doing afore this?'

'I was in the Forces. The army.'

'Ah,' Annie said. 'That why your hands shake?'

A bell jangled, shocking him. He turned in his chair and saw, above the door into the hall, a row of bells. The one labelled *Dining Room* was dancing on its little arm.

Annie swore softly. She stubbed out her cigarette on her plate. She went to the sink and took a tin of tooth-powder from the window ledge. She rubbed the powder over her teeth with a finger, ran the tap, sloshed water around her mouth and spat it out. She dried her hands on her apron and left the room.

After a minute, Martin reached for the wine.

Annie came back with Godley's tray and closed the door behind her with her foot.

'He'd like to talk to you. In the study. He wants to know if you'd like a small glass of port. He takes one himself, of an evening.'

She had two ways of speaking, two voices. One her own, one borrowed. He could not tell which was which. They bled into each other.

'Thank you. That would be nice.'

'I thought as much. Get on, then.'

Martin got to his feet.

Annie, with her back to him, said, 'He says he's minded to give you the job.'

'Ah.'

'He asked me if I thought you'd be suitable.'

'Did he? And what did you say?'

'I told him I didn have the faintest bloody idea.'

'Right.'

'You'd have to get ahold of your nerves.'

'I . . . yes.' He went to the door.

She said, 'I usually make a hot drink after I've got him to bed. About quarter past nine.'

'OK. Thanks.'

'*OK*,' she said, mimicking him in an approximately American accent.

It was entirely dark in the hall. Martin felt his way along the oak panelling towards a sliver of light.

5

ON THE SECOND DAY of May he moved into the groom's quarters on the upper floor of the stable block. They comprised four small rooms: a living room with a fireplace, a rudimentary kitchen, a bathroom with a claw-footed tub and, at the end of the passageway, a bedroom with a brass-railed bed. The ceilings sloped into the eaves.

The foolish word 'snug' came to him.

The living room and the bedroom each had a south-west-facing dormer window. They offered a view over the tall stone wall that separated Harold Godley's domain from a stretch of rough moorland pasture bisected by a bank of flinching hawthorn. Beyond that, layers of immeasurable distance.

It occurred to Martin, pleasurably, that he would be sleeping above the Phantom.

He unpacked his few things then noticed, hanging from a peg on the back of the door opening onto the narrow staircase, a black jacket and a black cap with a shiny peak. He tried them on. It was as if they'd been tailored for him. The only mirror in the flat was small and hung above the washstand in the bathroom. The man who stared out of it looked very unlike Martin Heath, and that too pleased him. He returned the chauffeur's kit to its peg and went down to the court-yard and through the back door of the house and into the kitchen. It was two thirty in the afternoon and he was hungry.

Mrs Maunder turned away from some greyish substance she was manhandling on a floured portion of the table.

'Ah, there you be, Mister Heath. Settled, then? I kep some soup back. Bowls over there, see? Spoons in that drawer. No, next one along. Thas it.' She used her head to gesture to the pan on top of the black cast-iron range. 'Help yourself. My hands is busy, as you see.'

He sat and ate. Root vegetable soup with a memory of chicken in it.

'This is delicious, Mrs Maunder. Thank you.'

It made her laugh. '*Delicious*,' she said. 'Oh, you'll fit right in. That's what *he* allers says, no matter what I scrapes together. I don't think he know one thing from'n other, but he allers says *Delicious, thank you, Mrs Maunder.*'

Since his arrival, Martin had not set eyes upon his new employer, nor Annie. Mrs Maunder had answered the door. She was a woman of indeterminate age and shape. Her eyes and smile belonged to a younger, less disappointed face. She had a gap in her front teeth. She wore a pinafore over a black dress and under a grey cardigan and, on her head, something Martin knew was called a mob cap because servants wore them in illustrated storybooks from his childhood.

Savouring the soup, it occurred to him that Mrs Maunder's existence was odd. Why would a very elderly man who ate, indiscriminately, tiny portions of food employ a full-time cook? He could not think of a way to broach the subject.

Mrs Maunder had produced a rolling pin from somewhere – somewhere about her person, perhaps – and was vigorously squashing the pastry with it.

Martin said, 'Have you worked for Mr Godley a long time, Mrs Maunder?'

The cook turned away from her work and aimed her rolling pin at him. Little swags hung from it like flayed skin.

'See yere,' she said. 'We can't be doin with this *Mister Heath* and this *Missus Maunder*. Not if you're meanin to stay. I wus christened Margaret, but prefer Peg for quickness. You?'

'Martin.'

Mrs Maunder nodded, grimacing humorously. Her expression suggested that being called Martin was a sore handicap to be endured with cheerful stoicism. She returned to her work.

'Well, *Martin*, lessee. I'll have been here twenty-one year come October.'

Which was, conversationally, something of a dead end. He tried again.

'It's none of my business, I suppose, but I was wondering how old Mr Godley is. He seems terribly . . . ancient.'

'He'd be eighty-somethun. Eighty-two or there'bouts.'

'He seems, well, very frail. And sad.'

She turned the flattened pastry over and slapped it down. She wiped her hands on her pinafore.

'He is,' she said. 'Specially this time of year. More soup?'

'No, I'm fine, thanks.'

'We didn' meet, first time you come here, cos you was late and I wus goin off. Did Annie say anythin to you?'

'Well, we . . . No, not really.'

'Her didn give you the lie of the land?'

The vaguely military phrase unnerved him.

'You mean as far as Mr Godley's concerned? No.'

'No. I don't suppose her would've.'

The cook sighed like a cushion heavily sat upon. Then she ferreted about in her pinafore pocket, eventually producing a heavy-looking fob watch. She squinted at it and stuffed it away again. It seemed to Martin that she might not say anything further.

So he said, 'Was he married? Does he have any children?'

These questions seemed to trouble her.

He said, 'I'm sorry. As I said, it's none of my business. It's just that . . .'

Peg Maunder's eyes darted to the kitchen door. He turned to see Annie standing there.

'Mr Godley sends his compliments,' she said by way of greeting. 'He's feelin tired an's gonter have a nap on the day bed. I'm to show you about the house, so's you know where's where and what's what.'

Her tone was flat, almost resentful. Martin stood up, perhaps too quickly, because it brought on the familiar moment of dizziness, of bright worms adrift inside his eyes. He held onto the back of his chair for a moment.

'Thank you,' he said.

Annie switched her gaze to the cook. 'Awright, Auntie?'

'As rain, maid. I'll put the kettle on for when you gets back.'

Like the study, the other downstairs rooms contained a superfluity of valuable and melancholic furniture. Most of it, Martin guessed, dated from the previous two centuries. The dining table would seat twelve, at least. He pictured the cadaverous old man sitting alone, picking at his skimpy meals.

'So Mrs Maunder's your aunt, is she?'

'Sort of. My mum's cousin.'

She led him towards the back door of the house. Just before she reached it she stopped and pulled open a door he had not noticed on his previous visit; under-standably, because, apart from a small handle, it was indistinguishable from the panelling that lined the hall. It opened onto a narrow flight of stairs.

'The back stairs,' Annie said. 'He like us to use'm to save the carpet.'

He followed her up, watching the muscles bunch in her calves.

At the top there was a small landing lit by a skylight. To the right, an even more narrow flight ascended into gloom. Ahead, another door which Annie pushed open. They emerged onto a green-carpeted corridor that ran the length of the building. Its dimness was punctuated by spills of light from two tall sash windows. Its walls were hung with black-framed etchings of classical ruins. Halfway along it, a pair of newel posts, their crowns carved into writhes of ivy, announced the arrival of the main staircase from the front hall. Annie walked briskly past them and opened a door.

'Mr Godley's bedroom,' she announced.

Martin followed her in. It was a very large room that contained, in addition to Godley's shadowy bed, a sofa and a matching pair of armchairs upholstered in vaguely medieval fabric, a mahogany commode, a dressing table upon which toiletries were reflected in a triptych mirror and a small leather-topped writing desk and chair in front of the bay window. Several small brown bottles and a glass on the bedside cabinet. The room's marble-tiled fireplace was empty and freshly cleaned.

Annie said, 'Mr Godley won't have fires lit upstairs after May Day. So there's a carryin job you've dodged.'

The window's heavy maroon curtains were half-parted; Martin caught a view of the drive and front lawns and, in the middle distance, the small cluster of Leeworthy's roofs and their protective trees.

Annie passed behind him and opened another disguised door, papered in the same brown-and-white pattern of rambling roses as the walls. 'Through here's his dressin room.'

Martin peered in and caught sight of himself in a cheval mirror.

'And through there's his bathroom. I made him promise never to lock it, just in case. But you can't allers trust him. Just so's you know.'

'OK.'

'I sit out here when he's havin a bath. He talks to me through the door so's I know he's all right. He's got a horror of havin one of his turns in the bath an drownin.'

Back out in the corridor Annie parked her bum on one of the two window ledges and said, 'There's five other bedrooms. No one's used them in years. Go an' have a look, if you like. I give'm a goin-over now an' again.'

The fourth door Martin opened revealed a room that slightly, and uneasily, reminded him of his own bedroom at his parents' house. A full bookcase on top of which a revolving globe stood. Age had given it a yellow patina, turning the world's oceans greenish. A single bed under an embroidered coverlet. In one corner, a cricket bat leaned against the wall, a dusty tasselled cap perched atop its handle. Pictures on the walls: a Nelson-era ship of the line under full sail, prints of elaborately uniformed hussars and dragoons. A framed photograph. Martin peered at it. Tiers of unsmiling boys stacked behind a seated row of black-gowned and bewhiskered schoolmasters. The lancet windows of a chapel in the background. Some of the older boys wore tasselled caps. Beneath the picture, in faded copperplate handwriting, *Charterhouse, 1911*.

He turned away and bleated a cry of alarm. There was a man standing behind the door. A soldier. Martin's breathing beat its wings in his chest. His brain flustered.

No, not a man. Not a real man. A tailor's dummy in army uniform. Khaki cap and long-skirted tunic, Sam Brown belt. Martin approached it, cautiously.

An officer's parade uniform from the 1914–18 war; a captain's, possibly. Medal ribbons, some of which he recognised. The faceless head was unbearable. Martin backed away and left the room, closing the door very carefully.

Annie was still sitting on the window ledge. She turned and looked at him with a smile on her face. Or smirk. He knew she'd heard the noise he'd made. He looked at her. Damned if he'd ask.

'His son's bedroom,' she said. 'Julian. Got himself killed in October 1918, three weeks afore the Armistice.'

'Cruel,' Martin said.

'Am I?'

He frowned, not knowing that he'd heard her correctly.

'Fate,' he said. 'I meant fate.'

'Oh. Yes. You'd think we'd learn, though, wouldn you?' She stood and went to the door to the servants' stairs and held it open.

He went through, then turned to her. 'And where do you . . . live?'

'Sleep, you mean?'

They were very close together in this small space. Annie sighed. 'Well, I s'pose you need to know where

I am, less anythin happen. Up above.' She tipped her head towards the narrower flight of stairs. 'You go first.'

He climbed, holding onto the thin metal handrail.

The servants' accommodation was a humbler and dimmer version of the floor beneath it.

'This here's my room,' Annie said, indicating the door closest to the stairs. 'I keep the door open at night, and the door onter the landin, so's I can hear if he calls out for me. He've also got a little bell next to the bed.'

'I see,' Martin said.

Annie leaned against the wall and folded her arms, looking down the passageway. 'Auntie Peg says all these rooms was used in the old days. Housekeeper an' her husband, three maids. Must've been a crush, I'd think.'

Martin nodded. He would have liked to look into her room, and wanting to do that made him angry with himself. He wanted to ask her if she ever felt lonely or afraid.

'So,' she said, 'are we done? I could murder a cuppa tea.'

Following her down the back stairs, Martin said, 'What about the rooms behind the kitchen? What are they?'

'Oh, scullery, cold room, coal hole, place where the pump was afore we got the water. You can have a poke about whenever you like.'

Late in the afternoon, Martin was sitting in his living room studying the Phantom's handbook. It was a daunting volume both in terms of its instructions, which were complex, and its tone, which was that of a stern and rather pompous schoolmaster. He was glad to be distracted by footfalls on the stairs. He went to the door. Annie was holding a shallow wooden box.

'We had a delivry. Man comes from the village, Fridays. There's bread an' eggs an' so forth for your breakfast.'

He took the box. 'Thanks.'

She went down the steps.

He said, 'Annie?'

'What?'

'I'm sorry you don't like me.'

'Don' I?'

'Don't you?'

'I haven't made my mind up on that score.' She looked up at him over her shoulder. 'There'll be food on the kitchen table at seven, if you want it.'

6

FOR SEVERAL WEEKS his nights were torture.

He'd driven the Morris van to Okehampton and had been directed to a doctor's surgery. It was a private house on George Street. The name on the brass plate beside the door was Bloom. He'd sat in the hallway, sharing a row of wooden chairs with doomed-looking older people and mothers with fractious children. He was the last person summonsed into the consulting room, a converted Georgian parlour into which an examination table and a skeleton had been inserted. Bloom was a man in his sixties with half-moon spectacles halfway down a disdainful nose. Martin told his tale.

'Well, Mister Heath. I sympathise, of course. However, certain, ah, difficulties present themselves. For a start, under the new regulations, you need to register with my practice before I can do anything at all. Have you done so?'

'No.'

'No. So what you must do is fill in this form. Then I can request your medical records from your previous doctor, and we can proceed from there.' He took a pen from the breast pocket of his waistcoat. 'The name of your previous doctor, Mister Heath?'

'I . . . I can't remember. It was a new doctor. A woman.'

'Really?'

'Yes. Before that it was Doctor McInnis. But he retired.'

'And this was in, ah, Blandford Forum, in Dorset?'

'Yes. You could look it up, I imagine.'

'Look it *up*, Mister Heath? I can't imagine what you mean.'

Martin looked down at the threadbare carpet between his feet. Sweat was beginning to prickle the skin on his back.

'Listen,' he said. 'I get nightmares. Really bad ones. In the daytime as well as at night. It's what they used to call shell shock. Look at my hands. I can't sleep. The pills helped. I know that you know what they were. Just give me some. Please.'

The doctor took his spectacles off and laid them on his desk. He leaned back in his chair. 'How much do you drink, Mister Heath?'

'What? Pardon?'

'How much do you drink? And what do you drink?'

Martin had twice persuaded the landlord of the Stag in Leeworthy to sell him a bottle of whisky at closing time. Knowing it was a bad idea. Word would reach Godley eventually, via Annie or Peg or the bloody postman or whatever or whoever. *Your chauffeur is an alcoholic, sir. Just thought you'd like to know.* So, apart from the glass of wine or two in the kitchen with Annie of an evening, he'd more or less stopped.

He told Bloom this and was disbelieved.

'Your, ah, lady doctor almost certainly prescribed you a form of barbiturate. Barbiturates in combination with alcohol can be lethal. I would be most reluctant to write you a further prescription for them, given your highly nervous condition. Instead, I recommend vigorous exercise. Long walks, for example. Or sessions of

PT before bedtime followed by a glass of warm milk.'

He opened a drawer of his desk and pushed a slim booklet across his desk.

'In my previous practice I treated several chaps who came back from the last war displaying symptoms similar to your own. There is, I'm sorry to tell you, no pharmaceutical antidote to horror. This little publication – I confess that I am its author – suggests a number of, ah, strategies that have proven helpful. It may surprise you to learn that playing cricket, for instance, is particularly effective. Do you play cricket, Mister Heath?'

The noise in Martin's head, the blood surf, had become intolerable. He stood and steadied himself.

'I was the first British NCO through the gates of Belsen. *Belsen*. Heard of it?'

'Yes. I happen to be Jewish, Mister Heath.'

Martin looked away from him, nodding. 'And I don't play fucking cricket,' he said.

He sat in the Morris's little cab for ten minutes before he could trust himself to drive.

Without pills and enough booze he became fragile after dark.

Harold Godley infiltrated his dreams and took possession of them.

The bald and breastless sleepwalking bone-woman had his head.

The wasted magnocephalic children listlessly awaiting death on the steps of the huts.

The desexed cadavers in the charnel pits, gurning up at him over their neighbours' ribcages.

They all had Godley's head.

At other times the heads had no faces at all, like the dummy wearing Julian Godley's uniform.

By such nocturnal instalments, Martin Heath's revulsion at his employer's deathly appearance modulated into disgust, then fear. It became increasingly difficult to disguise these emotions, to simulate the respect and deference that were part of his job. He knew that he ought to leave. But he had nowhere to go. Besides, when the ghosts left him alone he liked living at Burra Hall. The somewhat glum stolidness of the house appealed to him; its solitude, its furnishings, its stubborn unchanged existence all pretended that the murderous twentieth century had not occurred. Also, this was where the Phantom lived.

He imagined himself living here for ever. With

Annie. With the Rolls. Without Harold Godley.

When the nightmares were very bad he walked around the courtyard, smoking, like a prisoner taking exercise. From a position close to the gateway he could see Annie's bedroom window. Now and then he saw her vague silhouette traverse its thin curtain. On these occasions he imagined her naked, or nearly so.

On a night when tumultuous rain deterred him from the courtyard Martin went downstairs and followed the beam of his battery torch through the tack room and entered the coach house via the connecting door. The reflection of his torch in the Phantom's pale flank was a moon trembling through creamy cloud-haze. He climbed into the passenger compartment and settled himself on the sleek and yielding leather. He switched the torch off; then, after less than a minute, switched it on again, feeling a surge of anxiety. It seemed to him that Godley maintained a spectral presence in the car. That he was sitting at the other end of the seat. This was a foolish notion but also unbearable.

Martin got out and took up his proper position behind the steering wheel. That was better. Much better. In complete darkness he ran his fingers over the switches and dials. By now, his hands knew them; he silently recited their names. After a while he fell asleep.

The Godley-headed forms of death swarmed in but he didn't wake up.

He took to sitting in the Phantom a few nights every week, regardless of the weather, after Annie's light went out. He'd sleep for an hour or two behind the wheel and it was as if the latent power of the huge engine in front of him entered his unconsciousness and drove death away.

The lurid images paled. Dreams that were his own interceded. Dreams of sex with Annie. Dreams of killing death, of purging it.

He'd awake from these dreams tingling with a kind of impatience in the dark.

7

HE HELPED GODLEY into the Rolls. The old man had to get both feet on the running board before he could step in and more or less topple onto the back seat.

'Where to, sir?'

'Okehampton first, Martin. I have a prescription to be filled at the chemist's. There's also a small number of items I'd like you purchase on my behalf. I have a list. You might like to take the opportunity to stock up on cigarettes and so forth. And get me a copy of the *Telegraph* while you're at it.'

'Certainly, sir.'

July. Hot. The beeches either side of the road spread umbelliferous shadows through which sunlight flared and flickered. A man and his dog shrank into the hedge to let them pass. When he saw the kind of car it was he lifted his hat by way of salute.

Martin felt the now-familiar flowering of pleasure that driving the car brought him. The sense that he was not in charge of her. That he was following the flight of the silver girl. That the Phantom's huge intelligent engine was taking him somewhere better, somewhere unsoiled by his presence. With Godley's permission, he'd slid the roof of the driver's compartment open; green-scented air spooled in.

In Okehampton they parked close to the junction of Fore and Market streets. Immediately, a number of people gathered to admire the car. Martin, in shirt-sleeves today but wearing the cap, shifted to get out of the nearside door. Godley's tinny voice coming out of the speaker stopped him.

'I don't quite feel up to this, Martin.'

Martin twisted awkwardly to look into the passenger compartment. Godley hung the microphone back on its cradle and lowered the window blinds, then leaned forward and wound down the glass divider.

'Sir? Is anything the matter?'

'I shall stay in the car,' Godley said. He handed over two pieces of paper and a five-pound note. 'If you wouldn't mind.'

'Of course, sir.'

'Quick as you can, there's a good fellow. And shoo these people away.'

Martin ran the errands and returned to the car. The divider was still down.

'Home, sir?'

'No.' The old man's voice was the stirring of dry leaves. 'Go over the bridge and take the second turn on the right. I'll direct you.'

Martin drove cautiously. In many places the road between its mossy stone walls was barely wider than the Rolls. The thought of scraping her flanks was a horror to him. They juddered over a cattle grid.

'Here,' Godley said. 'Just ahead on the left.'

Martin eased the car off the road onto an uneven parking space, making sure that the rear door would open onto the gap between two black and sizeable puddles. It was strange that they were there; there had been no rain for almost three weeks. He made to get out and open the rear door.

Godley said, 'I'll stay inside, Martin. There's a chill in the air. But if you'd like to get out for a smoke, please do.'

'Thank you, sir.'

He walked five paces to the rear of the Rolls and lit up. He'd been driving on a twisting uphill gradient for several miles through dim green tunnels. Now, the open high moor stretched and folded away to great distances. To the west, a wall – a vertical jigsaw of stone – curved past an area of boggy ground in which big grassy hummocks stood like the heads of mad-haired giants buried upright; then it plunged down into a wooded cleave within which he could see the twinkle of water. Beyond this valley the land rose again, became an endless hill patchworked by more stone walls into gorsey paddocks in which sheep wandered, groaning. To the east, a plateau of grass and rocky outcrops fell away into farmland. The low tower of a church surrounded by a small jumble of roofs. Overhead, a lark – he tried to find it in the sky but could not – stitched the air with hectic music.

Martin ground his cigarette out with his heel and returned to the car, sliding back into his seat at the wheel. Godley had raised the blind on his window and was gazing out.

'I haven't been up here since before the war,' he said.

'It's a marvellous view, sir,' Martin said, reluctantly deploying troops in his head.

'Yes. You'd think nothing had happened.'

'Are you sure you don't want to get out, sir? It's quite warm, actually.'

The old man didn't respond. Martin's hands started to tremble. He gripped the steering wheel.

After a while Godley said, 'Are you settling in all right, Martin? It's been a while since we had a chat. I've been rather preoccupied.'

It had been a fortnight or so since they'd done more than exchange cursory greetings. Martin had taken instructions from Mrs Maunder and Annie or devised chores on his own initiative. Gates, the gardener, seemed to find him something of a nuisance and refused to remember his name. Now, it seemed, Godley wanted to talk. He usually did, in the Phantom.

'I'm perfectly happy, thank you, sir. No complaints.'

'You're feeling well, in yourself? Better, perhaps?'

He said, 'Yes, sir. Thank you.'

'And you're getting along with Annie?'

'I think so, yes.'

'Hmm. A good girl, but a bit of a cold fish, wouldn't you say?'

Martin didn't know how to respond.

'She grew up in Plymouth,' Godley said absently, as if he were speaking of an uninteresting fictional character. 'She was evacuated up here to her aunt's house in 'forty-one when the German air raids started in earnest. A week later, her parents' house took a direct hit. They were both killed. She was sixteen at the time. Has she told you any of this?'

'No, sir.'

'No. I'm not surprised. She's close, is Annie.'

Martin said nothing.

Godley said, 'I'm told that from up here you could see Plymouth burning.'

Then he fell silent. Martin risked a backwards look at him. He seemed near to death, as always.

'Sir? Shall I drive on?'

'No, not yet. Tell me, are you content with your accommodation? Hmm?'

'Yes, sir. I'm perfectly comfortable.'

'Good.'

After an eternity that lasted five minutes Godley turned away from the window, said, 'Enough, I think. Drive on, Martin.' He leaned forward and wound the divider up.

*

The beautiful car rose and dipped effortlessly along the road that seemed to have been built only for its pleasure.

And once again Martin pictured opening her up, unleashing her. Putting his foot hard down, making her roar, giving in to her. He imagined it precisely. On that stretch of the A30 the other side of Okehampton. At dawn. No other traffic.

Her huge bulk hurtling towards the sunrise, taking him with her. No Godley.

8

HE WAS MAKING a careful annotation in a margin of the Phantom's handbook when he heard the clatter on the stairs.

'Martin! Martin!'

He dragged the door open. 'Annie? What?'

She was frightened. Her hair was all over the place. Her apron was wet. 'I need you. Come to the house. Now. Don't just stand there. It's Mister Godley. Bloody come *on*!'

By the time he'd stuffed his feet into his shoes and gone down to the courtyard Annie had already vanished into the house. The late-evening sky was a mottle of apricot and purple.

The backstairs door was open.

'Annie?'

'Up here!'

The curtains in Godley's bedroom were drawn shut. Light tipped into the room from the open dressing-room door. Martin heard Annie say, 'Mr Godley! Mr Godley! Please wake up!'

He approached cautiously. Looked into the bathroom. Annie was bent over the bath.

From the doorway Martin said, 'What happened?'

'He's had one of his turns. All I did was go for a pee and when I come back he was face up under the water. Oh, *shit*! Mr Godley! Mr Godley!' She patted the old man's face.

'Is he dead?'

'I don't think so. I dragged him up and pulled the plug out soon as I saw him.'

'Have you called a doctor?'

'Course I bloody have. Be a half hour afore he gets here, though. Help me get him inter bed. I can't do it by myself.'

He stood, paralytic, looking down at Godley's dreadful body. The greyish lips pasted onto the skull, the ribcage of a stripped chicken, the little beige slug resting on the hairless crotch, the withered shanks.

Memory's claws emerged from its shell.

'Martin?'

His hands jittered but he could not move his legs. He was a condemned man standing on the scaffold's trap door.

'Martin!'

'I . . . I don't . . . I can't touch him.'

Annie straightened and turned to him. She studied his face for a second, then slapped it. It was not a fierce blow, but it brought tears to his eyes. '*Help* me,' she said.

He took a large towel from the rail and covered Godley's body with it. He went to the curved end of the bath, let out his breath in a little moan and got his hands under Godley's armpits.

He and Annie carried the old man to the bed.

God, he weighs almost nothing.

When Godley was decently covered and propped up on his pillows Annie held a small bottle under his nose. His eyelids flickered, he moved his head to the side and coughed.

'Thank Christ,' Annie said.

*

Martin could not stay in the room.

He sat on the lower flight of the front stairs. The hall was dark now. He attempted the impossible task of not thinking. When he heard tyres on the gravel he switched on the light and opened the door. It seemed to him that Bloom flinched slightly when their eyes met.

Martin made to lead the doctor upstairs but Bloom bustled past him.

'I know the way, thank you.'

Later, from the kitchen, Martin heard voices and the front door closing. He topped up his glass with wine and filled the other one. When Annie came in she sat down and drank half of it in a single draught. She helped herself to one of Martin's cigarettes and lit it with his lighter.

'Is he all right?'

She huffed smoke. 'As right as he'll ever be.'

'And you? Are you OK?'

'Yeah.'

It seemed to Martin that she was rather more than OK. Oddly, she did not appear to be either tired or strained. Sort of lit up. Thrilled, even. Perhaps she was a bit pleased with herself for managing the crisis, he thought. He wanted her.

She said, 'You went all to pieces again upstairs.'

There was nothing accusatory in the statement.

'Yes. I'm sorry.'

'You oughter talk to someone, you know.'

'What, like a head-doctor, you mean?'

She reached for the bottle so as to divert her gaze from his. 'Or me,' she said.

He drank some more Burgundy. When he managed to look at her again she was smiling, just a little.

She said, 'Change the subject?'

'Yes, please.'

'Go on then.'

Martin lit another cigarette. 'Do you ever think about what you'd do if, when, he dies?'

She looked at him levelly over her glass. 'Of course I do,' she said. 'All the time. Don't you?'

The following morning Annie climbed the stairs to Martin's flat and let herself in. He emerged from the bathroom only half-dressed, braces dangling, bearded with shaving suds.

'He wants you to sleep in the house from now on,' she said. 'After what happened last night.'

'Oh.'

'Just sleep. You don't have to move out of here.'

'OK.'

'Come over when you're ready and we'll sort you out.'

When she'd gone Martin stood in front of the mirror holding the razor, willing his hands to steady themselves.

He went up the back stairs to the top floor. Annie stood in the passageway with bedclothes in her arms.

'I preferred the previous arrangement,' she said.

'Yes. I'm sorry.'

They stood looking at each other for a moment until Annie said, 'Well, can't be helped. I'm putting you in the old housekeeper's room down the end. It's a bit bigger than the others.'

'Thanks,' he said, thinking, *And the furthest from yours.*

9

ON SUNDAYS AND occasional weekdays when he won time for himself, Martin took to hiking on the moor. His rucksack contained austere provisions – a hard-boiled egg, some bread and cheese, a flask of water – and one or two of the OS maps that shared a shelf of his bookcase with the Phantom's handbook and service record. He still liked maps, despite the use he'd put them to in recent years. He took pleasure in the names of Dartmoor's tors: Hound, Yes, Great Mis, Brat, Honeybag, Laughter.

Walking, gazing, he was often successful in

emptying his mind of thought and memory. He had a tactic: picturing his head as a glass cask of impure fluid draining from a spigot. Sometimes he would go for several hours without viewing the landscape as a battlefield, without assessing its possibilities for troop deployment. That damned quack, Bloom, had been right after all. Or partly right, anyway.

One afternoon in early September, after a long slow ascent through tall dense bracken, he found himself on a jutting ledge of granite overlooking infinite and interfolding swathes of ochre, gold and green. Distant sheep the size of maggots. There was a late-summer thickness to the air and he was sweating. He took off his shirt, folded it and sat down on it.

Halfway through his meagre rations he found himself considering the possibility of happiness. He considered the word cautiously; he'd had no occasion to use it for a very long time. He needed a reference for it. When had he last been happy?

This was dangerous territory. He'd invariably returned injured from forays into the past. But now, very quickly and unharmed, he found a boy – what, ten, a little older? – helping his mother pack a picnic hamper.

Of course, he thought, swallowing egg. *Picnic. That's what triggered this.*

The hamper was wonderful and ingenious. Wicker-work, with leather handles and straps. Inside it, at either end, cloth compartments of various sizes for plates, cutlery, tumblers, condiments, bottles. Inside the lid a sort of hammock that tablecloth and napkins could be tucked into. Martin had loved his mother's unvarying method of packing the hamper. The things you ate first had to be at the top. So, at the bottom, cheese and biscuits and a cake or tart covered with a teacloth. Then two kinds of sandwich and slices of a pork or chicken pie all neatly wrapped in grease-proof paper. Another teacloth, then tomatoes, lettuce, cucumber in a flat biscuit tin.

And this immutable ritual had made him happy.

Yes.

The hamper had been too big for the car's boot so Martin shared the back seat with it, listening to its creaky whispering on jolty sections of the road, inhaling its promises.

And now, brushing crumbs from his lap, he thought that perhaps happiness was a form of anticipation. Had he enjoyed the picnics themselves? He could not say. The memories – of where his parents had set up camp, of the eating down through the hamper's strata – were flickery and unreliable. He could not, now, stabilise or trust images of his mother, bothered by wasps, fussing over the arrangements. Or of his father, jacketless, his trilby angled to shade his eyes, propped on one elbow, smoking his pipe.

All gone into the land of ghosts.

He swigged water, lit a cigarette.

His father had considered extremes of emotion, especially in women, to be symptomatic of an underlying medical disorder. His mother, unwilling for her marriage to become a matter of ongoing diagnosis, had avoided displaying them. From his parents Martin had learned how not to demonstrate excitement or fear. This self-management had served him well at boarding school and, until close to its end, the war. The 'calmness under fire' for which he had been Mentioned in Dispatches was more a matter of fearing embarrassment than not fearing the enemy.

In so far as he'd thought about it at all, he'd assumed that people were equipped with, born with, a set of emotions just as they'd been given a set of organs. Hope, misery, fear, desire, love, etc. Lungs, kidneys, liver, eyes, a heart, etc. Alike, they were prone to disease, exhaustion, catastrophic failure. Some could be mended, restored, replenished. And some could not. The least little thing could make the difference.

The Phantom's engine had a V-twelve cylinder layout. Two banks of six cylinders turning a single crankshaft at the bottom of the V. Christ, a great beautiful complex lump of a thing. Twenty-four spark plugs bristling out of it. One of them fails, its partner takes over.

As for himself, he'd run out of pity but he couldn't fix it. It wouldn't spark. Its adjacent cylinder, disgust, was working fine.

But *happiness*?

Martin stubbed the thought out along with the cigarette and studied his map. If he could cut northwards down the gorse-dappled slope below him he could be back at Burra Hall in less than two hours by following the track of a railway for much of the distance. By now he knew that on Dartmoor the word 'railway' did not have its conventional meaning. Railways were not, usually, tracks along which a train would run. They were railed roadways, constructed by unimaginable labour, along which teams of horses would drag wagonloads of quarried stone to be used in the building of harbours, churches, bridges, sea defences.

Fifteen minutes later he came to a barbed-wire fence, slumped in places. A board bearing the faded words

Danger Deep Pits leaned against a post. He followed the downward curve of the wire until it turned sharply to the right where the ground dropped away. Now he saw that he'd been descending the rim of a vast gouge – a monstrous bite – taken out of the hillside. The sheer sides of this wound seeped water into a shadowy pool about fifty feet below him.

He tracked right, seeking a way down. The fence skirted another pit then gave up, grasping at a weathered wooden post at the rim of another excavation. It seemed to Martin, peering down, that this was a shaft of some sort, roughly circular. Beards of moss hung from its lip. He could not see the bottom of it. He picked up a stone and tossed it in, waiting for a splash or clatter. Neither came.

He negotiated his way around the hole and discovered a descent of crude steps, possibly man-made, probably not, and clambered down them. He found himself in a baffling complex of towering cliffs, cuttings, slopes of spoil and pools of water above which iridescent dragonflies hovered and darted. Only their hum and the trickle of water broke the dense silence. Here and there tracks, made by long-dead quarrymen or sheep, threaded their way up and along narrow grass-crested parapets.

Martin, his sense of direction lost, wandered through this desolation, seeking the railway. He climbed a low embankment and there it was, level and sensible, heading north and east alongside the quarry. Low ramps led up to it at intervals. Its rails had gone but stretches of sleepers, grey as stone, rusted bolts jutting from them, remained.

There was the rusted remains of a donkey engine, its smokestack aimed at the sky like an ancient howitzer.

A cluster of ruined stone buildings, roofless, the glassless windows gaping at the moor.

He stood motionless, feeling the sweat trickle down his back.

He'd been here before, many times. Walked though trashed villages just like these.

Cradling the Thompson sub-machine gun in his arms. Following the point man – what was his name? Bentham? Bentley? – from whom fear radiated like the green light of radar. Which was why he was good.

Through the rubble of places called *Santo* something or *Saint* something. Signalling the rest of the patrol to wait, come ahead, wait, overlap. Studying lopped towers of churches through the field glasses, looking for the shadow or glint of a sniper.

A bicycle folded double by a half-track.

An eviscerated horse between the shafts of a toppled cart.

Houses improbably intact among the rubble. Pushing open the door of one to see a black veil of flies lifting from a dead boy's face.

That idiot Jackman grabbing up a booby-trapped album of pornographic postcards. His severed head, still grinning, bouncing on the cobbles.

He squinched his eyes shut, driving it all back into darkness. Turned round before opening them again, needing to open them because the whirring pits of dizziness were opening at his feet. He made his legs take him along the dismantled railway. After stumbling two hundred yards or so he felt more or less all right again and stopped to light a cigarette. He inhaled, swearing at himself. He looked to his left and was surprised to see, beyond a pair of padlocked iron gates, a narrow metalled road.

He shrugged the rucksack off and took out the map. Two faintly dotted parallel lines indicated a walking track running alongside the railway for a mile or so before veering away northwards. As far as he could make out, it joined, five miles or so out of Burra, a back road winding between Leeworthy and Lydford.

Sometime after the map had been drawn – during the war, probably – this track had been tarmacked. Turned into something you could drive along.

He walked on briskly, heading for what he now called home, keeping his eye on the road until it parted company with the railway.

On the following Sunday, with the map on his lap, he drove the Morris van out of Burra. At an unmarked junction he turned left and after twenty minutes, during which he met or saw no other vehicle or human being, passed the quarry's padlocked gates. Three miles beyond them, the road ended at a little huddle of buildings perched on a bare hill. Military buildings, obviously. Low huts made of prefabricated concrete sections under curved corrugated-iron roofs.

Martin parked the van and went to investigate, although it was clear that the place had been abandoned. Two of the buildings were doorless. He looked into the first one he came to. It was empty and intensely cheerless, pellets of sheep shit scattered over its concrete floor.

He walked around the site. Six slabs of concrete into which eyelets for guy-wires were set suggested that a radio mast had been the purpose of the place. He imagined the poor bastards manning it up here in the winter.

He returned to the Morris and drove back to the quarry. The gates were chest-high and easily clambered over. He had some difficulty orienting himself, but eventually he found his way to the depthless shaft. He chose a larger stone this time. It vanished without a sound. He did it again.

Then he lay on his back with his head resting on his hands and watched the slow reconfiguring of the clouds, thinking. Dreaming.

PART TWO

Something Apparently
Inconsequential

May 1948

1

SERGEANT ARCHIBALD BULLER of the Okehampton station, Devon County Constabulary, stood
by his car for a moment to admire the proportions
of Burra Hall, which this morning were enhanced by
spring sunlight. Before he could knock on the door it
was opened by a distraught young woman.

'Have you found him? Is he all right?'

'No news yet, miss, I'm afraid. May I come in?'

In the kitchen he introduced himself to Martin
Heath, who looked like he'd had a sleepless night and
was in need of a shave.

'We've sent a Missing Persons Alert to all stations,' the sergeant said, 'and we've contacted Exeter City police. That's as much as we can do for the time being.'

Annie Luscombe moaned softly and went to lean against the sink where she stood, sniffing and chewing a thumbnail. Buller sat himself at the table and took out his notebook. Martin Heath, who had been pacing the room smoking, sat down opposite. Buller noted the tremor in the chauffeur's hand when he lifted the cigarette to his mouth.

'I need to go through the details with you, if you don't mind. You say you drove Mr Godley to Okehampton where he took the one-fifteen train yesterday to Exeter for an appointment with his solicitor. Is that right?'

'Yes.'

'And the name of this solicitor, Mr Heath?'

'I . . . I'm afraid I don't know. I don't think he ever mentioned the name to me.'

'I see. Do you happen to know, Miss Luscombe?'

'I'm sorry, I . . . There might be something in his study, I s'pose.'

'Right-oh. Perhaps we could take a look in there in a minute.' He turned back to Martin. 'And he, Mr Godley, told you to meet him off the return train, the four thirty from Exeter.'

'Yes. But he wasn't on it.'

'So what did you do?'

'Well, I assumed he'd missed it for some reason. So I waited for the next one, but he wasn't on that, either. So I drove back here. I thought perhaps Mr Godley might have phoned Annie, Miss Luscombe, with a message or something. But he hadn't. I drove back to Okehampton in case he was on the last train, the nine o'clock. When he wasn't on that, I went to the police station.'

'Where you explained the situation to the night duty officer and provided a description of Mr Godley. A very detailed and useful description, if I may say so. All the same, a recent photograph of Mr Godley would be very useful. Is there one somewhere?'

'I don't know. Annie?'

She had, it seemed, become distracted by anxiety. 'What? Pardon?'

'The sergeant wants to know if there's a recent photo of Mr Godley anywhere.'

'I shouldn't think so. I don' think he've had his picture taken since I've been here. Not that I know of.'

She watched disapprovingly while Sergeant Buller poked about in the study. There were no photographs of any sort on the mantelpiece or the shelves, a fact that Martin had not previously registered. There was no correspondence lying about and the large bureau was locked.

Martin said, 'Look, um, Mr Godley is not in the best of health. He has, well, attacks. Fainting fits. He might have collapsed and . . .'

'Yes. I called the Royal Devon and Exeter first thing this morning. Three elderly gentlemen were admitted during the past twelve hours. They were all conscious and confirmed their names. None of them was your Mr Godley.'

Detective Inspector Ivan Sheepstone, a Yorkshireman, had an inordinate fondness for Cornish pasties. Nowadays, of course, they weren't a patch on the pre-war ones. Mostly potato and swede, and such molecules of meat as they contained were of doubtful provenance. Still, Carr's Bakery made a fairly decent one, all things considered; well-seasoned, with a tawny coxcomb of crisp pastry. Sheepstone was halfway through one of these delicacies, with his handkerchief spread on the desktop to catch the crumbs, when Detective Sergeant Raymond Panter's head poked round the office door.

'Sir? Just had a call from Exmouth. Seems one of the locals was doing a spot of fishing early this morning and found a pile of clothes on the beach.'

'Uh-hmm?'

'Well, sir, it seems to me that they might fit the description of what that old boy was wearing. The one that's gone missing. Godfrey.'

'Godley.'

'Yessir. Black coat, grey hat and scarf. And a walking stick.'

Sheepstone extracted something fibrous from his teeth and examined it forensically. 'Well,' he said, 'it's a nice enough day for a trip to the seaside. Call Exmouth back and tell them we're on our way. Oh, and Ray? Tell them I'll want to talk to the chap who found the clothing.'

He was a bearded and burly man in his forties. His name was George Rowsell. He happened to be the brother of PC Arthur Rowsell of the Exmouth station, the fourth member of the group gathered on the beach.

'And this is the exact place, Mr Rowsell?'

'Yup.'

Sheepstone gazed out over the water. Far away to his right, the green undulations of Lyme Bay's western coast folded into the distance. A plume of train smoke doodled along its edge. To his left, some half a mile away, the ragged ledges of Orcombe Point descended to the sea, the red sandstone in this light the colour of raw beef. Overhead, peevish herring gulls sought balance on the stiff breeze.

'How can you be sure, Mr Rowsell?'

'I fish from this spot reg'lar. Tis where the deep water channel come closest to the beach, see? Tha's why if he went in here yesday afternoon, well, he could be anywhere by now, miles along the coast. Might never find'n at all.'

Panter said, 'Why do you say that?'

'Like I say, the deep water come in right close here. See that sandbar fifty yard off? When the tide's goin out, the whole est'ry empty out atween that an' the beach. Tis like a funnel. The water come through here faster'n a man can run. Helluvan undertow an' all. There's bin several few drowned over the years, daft enough to go inter the water here. There was that boy swept out back in thirty-seven, wun't it, Arthur? We never found'n.'

'We?'

PC Rowsell said, 'Me'n George're with the lifeboat.'

'Right,' Sheepstone said. 'And the tide was going out yesterday afternoon?'

'Yup. Low water was just afore six.'

'Have you alerted the Coastguard, Constable?'

'I have, sir. As far as Weymouth.'

'Good. Tell me, Mr Rowsell, how was the clothing arranged when you found it?'

'Very neat, sir. Coat folded just so, scarf folded on top of that, shoes on top of the scarf side by side like in a shop. Glasses inside one of the shoes. Hat an' stick longside. The hat were upside-down with a stone in it. Twas like he meant to come back fr'um.'

The staff at Exmouth railway station were less than helpful. The stationmaster, a rather bumptious fellow with an ill-advised moustache, told the detectives that he normally had business with the train driver or the guard that denied him the luxury of scrutinising disembarking passengers. The ticket collector thought he might have seen an old man in a black coat getting off the four o'clock, but he couldn't be rightly sure.

Panter opined, driving back to Okehampton, that the ticket collector was 'a brick or two short of the full load anyway'.

2

LATE IN THE AFTERNOON Martin Heath was running a chamois leather over the Phantom's glass-work when he was distracted by an appreciative wolf whistle. A man he'd never seen before, but had been expecting, stood just outside the coach house's open doors with his hands in the pockets of his raincoat.

The man said, 'Hell's teeth. A Rolls. What a beauty.'

'Yes,' Martin said. 'A Rolls-Royce Phantom Three Sedanca de Ville, to be precise. Are you from the police?

Your Sergeant Buller was here this morning . . .'

The man produced and briefly displayed a warrant card. 'Detective Sergeant Raymond Panter, Devon County Constabulary. You are Mr Martin Heath?'

'Yes.'

'And you drive this thing, do you?'

'Yes, sometimes.'

'Lucky beggar. I've never even seen one before.'

'Have you found Mr Godley?'

'I wonder if you'd mind coming over to the house. My superior officer would like a word.'

The clothes and shoes, the cane and the spectacles, were displayed on the kitchen table. Annie looked up at Martin, white-faced, when he came in. The tall man with thick greying hair and a Yorkshire accent introduced himself.

Then he said, 'Mr Heath, I'd like you to examine these items carefully and tell me whether or not they belong to your employer.'

Martin lifted a shaky hand to his face and said, 'Oh, Jesus.'

'Mr Heath?'

'They're his. Where did you find them?'

'Please examine them more closely, Mr Heath.'

Martin approached the table, but could not bring himself to touch anything. His hands dithered. 'They're his,' he said.

Sheepstone said, 'You are absolutely sure that these are your employer's clothes and that he was wearing them when you last saw him? And that this is his walking stick?'

'Yes.'

Annie said, 'Oh, Martin.'

He said, 'Where did you find them?'

Panter said, 'They were discovered on the beach at Exmouth early this morning.'

'Exmouth?'

'Yes.'

Annie said, 'They think Mr Godley drowned himself. In the sea.'

Martin lifted his head, frowning. 'That's, that's ridiculous. Why would he do that?'

Sheepstone said, 'Well, we're hoping that you might help us find the answer to that question.'

'No,' Martin said. 'No, no, *no*. I took Mr Godley to the station because he had an appointment in Exeter. He was his normal self. He told me to meet him off the return train.' He gestured at the table. 'This is some sort of mistake. Obviously. I mean, how would Mr

Godley have got to Exmouth, of all places? It doesn't make any sense.'

'We're working on the assumption that he took the train on from Exeter to Exmouth, although we are unable to positively confirm that.'

'No. I don't believe it. He would have said something. He's very . . . particular.'

'Did he say anything at all to you, Mr Heath? Did you have any conversation in the car?'

'Not really. He said something about the weather. He asked me to fetch his travel blanket before we set off. He feels the cold.'

'And at the station? Did he say anything to you before getting on the train?'

'Only to confirm the time I was to pick him up.'

'I see. Um, this morning you told Sergeant Buller you couldn't recall the name of Mr Godley's solicitor in Exeter. I don't suppose it's come to either of you?'

'No, I'm sorry. I'm pretty sure he's never mentioned it to me.'

'Miss Luscombe?'

Annie shook her head.

'Well, thank you both. I'm sure this is all very distressing for you. Either DS Panter or myself would like to call by tomorrow morning for a word with your cook. Mrs Maunder, is it? Say ten o'clock?'

'She mightn't be here,' Annie said. 'Lily took a turn for the worse and she've taken a couple of days off to look after her.'

'Lily?'

'Her sister, my other auntie. She's a poor old thing. She've been under the doctor for years.'

Panter hid a smile behind his hand.

Sheepstone said, 'So she, Mrs Maunder, wasn't here yesterday?'

'No. She's not been in since last Saturday. Don' think as she'll likely be back till Monday.'

'Right. Well, if she *does* come in tomorrow, would you mind ringing the number Sergeant Buller gave you? Oh, and speaking of doctors, do you know who Mr Godley's is?'

'Bloom,' Martin said. 'In George Street.'

In the Wolseley Panter said, 'If I was thinking of doing away with myself, I wouldn't choose drowning. Bloody awful. And too slow, I'd think. You'd have time to think better of it. I have to admit, looking at that sea gave me the willies. Poor old sod.'

'Hardly poor, Ray.'

'True, sir. You should see the Roller in his garage. Beautiful thing. Huge.'

'Yes, I've seen it around town a few times.'

Sheepstone was silent for half a mile, then he said, 'The stone in the hat was a bit rum, don't you think? Why would you put a stone in your hat?'

'To stop it blowing away, I suppose.'

'Yes. Odd, though, isn't it? Why would he bother?' He looked at his watch. 'Nearly five. Let's call it a day. First thing tomorrow, get on the blower and call all the solicitors in the Exeter directory. Find out who represented Godley. If they want to know why you're asking, say it's a police matter and say nowt. While you're doing that I'll go and have a word with Simon Bloom.'

'Right, sir.'

'Now then, I reckon we could persuade Brian at the White Hart to serve us a pint in the back room, don't you?'

3

'I APPRECIATE THE NEED for doctor-patient confidentiality, of course,' Sheepstone said, 'but in the circumstances . . .'

Bloom palpated his lower lip with his forefinger, frowning. Sheepstone waited.

Eventually the doctor sighed and said, 'Well, it's no secret that Harold Godley is not in the best of health. However, his, ah, complaints are not uncommon among people of his age. They are manageable with the proper medication.'

'It was more his mental state I was wondering about.'

'You're pushing it, Ivan.'

'Aye, I know.'

'But in the circumstances.'

'Yes. Your patient may have come to harm.'

'Harold is an unhappy man, and with good reason. But he is not, in my opinion, *depressed* in the clinical sense of the term. If you're asking me if he had suicidal tendencies, I'd say no. In fact, it's quite rare for elderly people to commit suicide.'

'Is it?'

'Yes. But' – Bloom spread his hands – 'who knows? A moment of acute despair, something apparently inconsequential that tips us over the edge. These things are not predictable.'

'No. Well, thanks, Simon. I'll let you get on.' Sheepstone stood and turned to the door. 'Oh, one last thing, while I'm pushing my luck. I take it that Mr Godley was on regular medication?'

'Yes. And now you're going to ask me if anything he was taking could be lethal. And the answer is yes, theoretically. A large overdose, especially if combined with alcohol, could cause liver failure. Almost certainly would do, in a person of Harold's age and condition. Were there empty bottles of any sort found with his things?'

'No.'

Bloom shrugged and said, 'Well, there you are. You'll keep me posted, Ivan, will you? I was rather fond of the poor old bugger.'

After a brief stop at Carr's Bakery, Sheepstone returned to the station where he found DS Panter looking rather pleased with himself. Almost gleeful, in fact.

'Got it fourth time of asking, sir. Earnshaw and Browning, offices on Southernhay. A Mister Jonathan Browning is Godley's solicitor.'

'Good. I suppose we'd better make an appointment. They probably won't take kindly to us dropping by un-announced.'

'The thing is, sir, Godley didn't have an appointment on Wednesday afternoon.'

'He didn't?'

'No, sir. And the secretary or whatever she was said she'd certainly have seen him if he'd been there. She said that in any case, Browning was at the County Court all day Wednesday.'

'Ah.'

Panter waited.

Sheepstone said, 'Get someone to make a cuppa, would you?'

'Sir. Oh, and Archie would like a word. Shall I send him in?'

Sergeant Buller came on in and got straight to the point. 'As requested, sir, I interviewed Jim Bolsover yesterday afternoon,' Buller said.

'Who?'

'The stationmaster here. He confirms everything that Heath told me. Godley bought a first-class return to Exeter – well, Heath bought it for him, to be exact – and Bolsover saw him help the old boy onto the train. He also spoke to Heath late afternoon, after Godley had failed to turn up. Said he seemed very agitated.'

'Yes. Bit of a nervy type, I'd say.'

'Yes, sir.'

'OK, Archie. Thanks.'

Sheepstone returned to his pasty.

'There's one other thing, sir. It mightn't have anything to do with anything, but, well, soon as I heard the name Godley it gave me a little itch in the head and I've only just now been able to scratch it. It was talking to Jim Bolsover that did it.'

Sheepstone chewed, patiently.

'You see, sir, Jim's father Harold – passed away oh, five or six years ago, now – he used to be sergeant here when I joined the force. And I remembered something he told me about Mr Godley's wife. So when I got back here I looked it up in the files.'

'The suspense is killing me, Archie.'

'She committed suicide, sir. Drowned herself.'

'Did she, indeed? When was this?'

'Eleanor Godley went missing on May the fourth 1920. Her body was retrieved from the Okement reservoir the following day.'

'And it wasn't an accident?'

'No, sir. She left a note. Posted it to her husband from the village. I reckon he'd have read it about the same time she was being fished out.'

'Hell's bells. Poor bastard.'

'Yessir.'

'Well, that's interesting, Archie. Thanks. Is that tea brewed yet?'

4

ON SATURDAY MORNING Ivan Sheepstone completed his solitary breakfast and, over a cup of tea, considered the day ahead. A couple of hours in the office: he needed to get back to that breaking and entering in Chagford, from which the Godley business had distracted him. Ridiculous, the valuable stuff people in this part of the world left lying around.

Lunchtime, a couple of pints. Then, the weather holding up so well, go and watch Okehampton Argyle. Kick-and-rush stuff, it'd be – Sheepstone was a devotee of Sheffield Wednesday – but it would be an entertaining enough interlude before the emptiness of the evening. Maybe Ray might fancy the game too. If his pregnant and possessive wife would let him off the leash.

He was putting on his bicycle clips when the phone rang.

'Yes? Hello, Ray. Yes, I am. I'm just about to leave. Five minutes then.'

Panter, when he arrived, looked satisfied with the information he had to impart.

'Constable Rowsell in Exmouth,' he reported, 'says a number of people responded to the appeal in the *Western Morning News*. Two were able to give pretty detailed descriptions that match Godley. Rowsell is writing up their statements. They should get to us by Monday.'

'Where and when did they see him, exactly?'

'A chap working in the public gardens saw him go past. And those gardens are on the way from the railway station to the seafront. He thinks it would have been about four o'clock. He knocked off at half past. Then a woman is sure she passed him on her bike about a hundred yards east of the lifeboat station.'

'Time?'

'She said somewhere between four and four thirty as well.'

Panter looked at Sheepstone expectantly. 'That seems to tie things up, sir, I'd say.'

'It would seem to. And you know what that means, don't you, Ray?'

'Yeah. I've got typing to do.'

'Fraid so. Leave it till Monday, though. We'll need to take a formal statement from wossisface, Heath, before you get started anyway.'

Something in Sheepstone's voice caused Panter to hesitate before leaving the room. 'Something bothering you, sir?'

The inspector sighed. 'I'd like to get this sorry business wrapped up as much as you would, Ray. But it's still open-ended, isn't it? We've no body, no suicide note. Therefore we can't hand it over to the coroner, much as I'd like to. Technically, we're still investigating a missing persons case.'

'True, sir, but . . .'

'Yes, I know.' Sheepstone looked up, cheered up. 'Fancy a jar at lunch time? Then the footie? Argyle are playing Princetown. Local derby. Last game of the season. It might be a bloodbath.'

The sergeant sucked a breath through his teeth, ruefully. 'No can do, sir. Irene's got me papering the baby's bedroom.'

'Of course.'

Panter, weighing his interests, said, 'I dare say I could manage a swift one, though.'

'Good. Knock on my door at twelve thirty.'

'Could we make it twelve fifteen, sir?'

'We could, Ray. By all means.'

PART THREE

You Fit My
Wounds Exactly

May 1948

1

IN THE COACH HOUSE Martin Heath sat behind the wheel of the Rolls-Royce thinking about the way the old man had died. He knew, of course, that it would stay with him for ever. In vivid and cinematic detail. But – although it was early days yet, be careful – it had driven out the other images that had monstered his dreams. As he'd hoped – no, been sure – that it would.

Godley had taken them with him.

In fact, Martin realised with a joyous sense of relief, of release, he could now safely conjure up Godley's death-mask face without releasing those other ghouls from their oubliette. He did so now. It brought no horrors with it.

It was strange, wonderfully strange, that he could even recall the dreadful moment when he had realised the old man was awake without the memory sending a tremor through his body. He took his hands from the wheel and looked at them. Steady as a rock.

He'd assumed the bedroom would be in darkness. It hadn't been. A little oil lamp burned on the bedside table beneath a shallow dish that was the source of the sweetly astringent smell that filled the room. He remembered it from his childhood. Eucalyptus.

Excellent for clearing the nasal passages, Martin.

I don't like it, Daddy.

Sssh. Go to sleep.

Tiptoed in his socks towards the foot of Godley's bed.

A pillow he could ease away without waking him up.

'Hello, Martin.'

He stood, frozen. Couldn't make himself advance. Too late to retreat. He thought for a moment or two he had imagined the voice: the old man seemed to be asleep.

Then the little lamp flared slightly and Martin saw the glitter of Godley's half-opened eyes.

'Is this it, at last, Martin? I've been waiting for quite a long time.'

The voice was drowsy. The sleeping pill. Maybe more than one.

Martin couldn't speak. Talking had not been part of it. He thought that perhaps he could leave the room, that in the morning the old man would think he'd dreamed it. But he still could not move.

'One last thing I want you to do for me. Are you listening?'

'Yes, sir.'

'Go to my son's room. Fetch his uniform.'

'What?'

'Just do it, please. I won't ring for Annie while you're gone. Be no point anyway, would there?'

He walked down the dark corridor. The whole fucking thing was too appalling. He couldn't breathe properly. In the dead boy's room he fumbled with the tunic's buttons, gasping. Tore it free of the faceless mannequin. Carried it and the cap to Godley's bedroom. The corridor had doubled in length. He thought his legs might give out.

'Put it on,' Godley said.

'No.'

'Please. It's the last thing I shall ever ask of you.'

The tunic was a size too small. He couldn't manage all the buttons. The cap fitted.

'Come closer.'

Martin approached the bed and made himself look down at the old man. Godley's eyes opened wider and he began to cry.

'My poor dear boy. I am so sorry. So very sorry. Can you forgive me? Are you generous enough to do that?' He sobbed in a breath. 'Are you *brave* enough?'

No, Martin thought. *I'm not. I can't do it. I'm too weak*.

But then Godley lifted his head. His yellow eyes glared into Martin's. Something that might have been a smile twisted his lips, but when he spoke his last words they were harsh. Fierce.

'No. Because you hate me!'

And at last Martin felt the necessary violence. It burned through him like a bullet. He climbed onto the bed, knelt astride the old man and pressed the pillow down over his face. He stiffened his arms, leaning all his weight into them. He watched Godley's hands crawl free of the bedclothes. They fastened onto the arms of the tunic. It seemed to Martin that they were trying to drag him down, not push him away. He felt Godley's legs lift and try to walk, then fall, then jiggle, then stop. The hands fell away. Martin continued to force the pillow down until his arms began to vibrate with the effort.

He straightened his back and when his breathing had steadied he reached under the pillow and felt for a pulse in the old man's neck. There wasn't one.

He got off the bed, went to the window and raised the sash. Cool damp air. He smoked a cigarette. The flame didn't tremble when he lit it.

Through the Phantom's windscreen he watched a mob of sparrows conduct lively business among the ivy covering the courtyard's far wall.

He ought, of course, to banish the memory to some secluded part of his mind. Build a wall around it, dig a moat around the wall. The best liars are those who have exiled the truth. Their tongues don't slip.

That copper with the Yorkshire accent had made him edgy.

It was all right, though. He had put Godley on the train and that was it. Beyond that he knew nothing. He was as baffled as everyone else.

Yes, it was all right. Nothing had gone wrong, he was sure of it. It had worked like a dream.

He looked at his watch. A bit early for a drink, but what the hell. He reached across to the door handle. A light click came from the loudspeaker.

Then: 'Hello, Martin.'

His breath and heart came to a halt.

'How are you today, Martin?'

It was a terrible effort to lift his head and look into the rear-view mirror. In which he saw Harold Godley smiling at him, holding the microphone.

Martin shoved the door open and more or less fell out of the car and stumbled into the courtyard. The sparrows skirled out of the ivy. He walked on unreliable legs to the gateway and through it. He stopped then and put his hand on the wall to support himself. His heart struggled. He made himself walk onward into the kitchen garden. A fork left standing in the black soil. A heap of horse manure. They didn't seem real. The afternoon light wasn't coming from the sky. It was electrical, artificial.

He sat on the wrought-iron bench beyond the flower beds and after a passage of time and two cigarettes managed some semblance of self-control. He was still shivering but that was because he was, in fact, cold. Shadow was advancing into the garden from the foot of its western wall.

There were only two possibilities. The first – that he had gone mad, that his brain had finally gone completely fucking haywire – he angrily dismissed because it would be so cruelly unfair. Now, after all he'd done. After he'd purged the darkness from his mind. It would be like getting killed by a stray bullet after victory had been bloodily achieved. He'd seen that happen. It could not happen to him. He would not let it.

The other explanation, the rational one, was that he'd been reliving Godley's death, and because it had been so vivid in his memory his mind had played a trick on him. What he'd seen in the mirror, heard from the speaker, were merely hallucinations. Yes. He'd had them before.

So what he had to do was get a grip on himself and go back to the Phantom.

The interior of the coach house had dimmed. Martin switched on the wall lights. He made himself walk around the car and look into the rear windows. All he could see was his own reflection. When he came round to the open driver's door he hesitated for a despairing moment then leaned in. He peered through the glass partition into the passenger compartment which was, of course, unoccupied. He got into his seat and held the wheel, staring straight ahead. He would not think about Godley. Nor would he think about the letter he'd received from his mother that morning containing two mentions of her new 'friend'.

No, he would think about Annie. Not his mother. Not Godley.

An icy thrill ran through his bladder when the speaker clicked.

'I am sorry that I alarmed you, Martin. Please remain in the car. I mean you no harm, I assure you.'

Martin refused to look in the mirror.

Godley said, 'I'm going to wind the divider down.'

Martin heard the glass whisper down into its recess. His grip on the wheel tightened. A rat scuttled about inside his chest.

'That's better,' Godley said. 'Now we can talk.'

'You are not real.'

'Am I not? I feel quite real at the moment.'

'You are a figment of my imagination.'

Godley clucked his dry little laugh. 'Oh no, Martin. It's not as bad as that. Don't think that.'

'You're dead.'

'Indeed I am. You'd know that better than anyone. You made a sturdy job of it, if I may say so.'

Martin forced himself to glance at the mirror. Only

the right side of Godley's face was illuminated by one of the wall lamps. But he was substantial enough and still smiling.

Soundlessly, Martin began to cry. Godley's smile faded into dismay.

'Please, Martin. Corporal Heath.'

'What do you want?'

'To go for a drive, of course. No, not now. You're not up to it and the light is fading. Besides, Annie will be wondering where you've got to. Tomorrow morning. There are things we need to discuss.'

'No. You're not real. Fuck off. Leave me alone.'

The leather of the rear seat creaked softly. Something light and warm settled onto Martin's shoulder, bringing with it the scent of eucalyptus. He cried out and shuddered away from it.

'Tomorrow, Martin. Ah, here's Annie now.'

She stood in the doorway with a cardigan over her shoulders. 'Martin?'

He wiped his eyes quickly and wound down the window. She came to it and looked in at him.

'I was wondering where you'd got to. What're you doing?'

'Nothing. Thinking.'

'Well, stop it, then. Come indoors.'

'OK. I'll lock up.'

The mirror reflected the vacant passenger compartment.

When he came into the kitchen Annie clanked the range door shut and straightened up. 'What's the matter?'

'Nothing. I'm fine.'

'You don't look it.'

'Really. I'm OK.'

'Hmm. I reckon I know what you need.'

She left the room and returned a minute later with a bottle in her hand.

'Here,' she said. 'This'll put some lead in yer pencil. Get the corkscrew.'

2

MARTIN HAULED the coach-house doors open but did not get into the car or look into it. He went to the big metal tank at the back of the coach house and filled the two-gallon watering can with petrol.

Dead-Not-Dead Godley's voice from a year ago in his head:

'As soon as Chamberlain came back from his little *tête-a tête* with Hitler in Munich and waved that scrap of paper in the air I knew that war was inevitable, Martin. So I had the tank installed and filled with three hundred gallons of petrol. In the nick of time, as it turned out. The Phantom is thirsty, as you know. Eight and half miles per gallon, on an easy run. How much is left, would you say?'

He'd squinted at the level in the glass tube. 'Just over a hundred, I'd say, sir.'

'That's what I'd have thought. We haven't stretched the old girl's legs much these past years.'

Now, he lugged the can five times to the Phantom and gurgled the juice into her. Then he went up to his flat and washed his hands and face without looking in the bathroom mirror and put the cap and jacket on. He went back down the stairs and got into the driving seat of the car. The divider was down.

Godley said, 'Thank you for dressing appropriately, Martin.'

'All right. All *right*. You're in my fucking head. So be it. Where d'you want to go?'

'Do you feel able to drive competently, Martin?'

'Yes.'

'I do hope so. We'd both be most unhappy if you damaged the car.'

'I'm all right.'

'Good. Do you know how to get to the Okement reservoir?'

*

He eased the Phantom down the lumpy service road and parked close to a windowless brick building from which a huge flanged pipe protruded then plunged into the ground. He hesitated, not knowing if he was supposed to hold the rear door open. Godley didn't speak. When Martin looked in the mirror there was no one in it.

He got out of the car and lit a cigarette. A path of muddy gravel sloped down towards the reservoir's margin, then turned and vanished behind greening birches and a tumble of rock. He walked to the periphery of the parking space and the dam came into view: a vast bulwark of granite blocks slanting out of the water. A balustraded walkway ran along the top of it. Godley was standing at its mid-point, his hands on the rail, gazing out over the lake. A pair of hikers passed him without a glance. Martin tried to hold his mind steady, as if it were something that might spill.

He ground the cigarette out and returned to the Phantom. After a minute or so he felt a momentary draught on the back of his neck, caught a hint of eucalyptus. In the mirror he watched Godley settle himself in the familiar, fussy, way.

'Now then, Martin. There are things you need to know.'

'Are there?' He'd managed to sound ironic, and Godley caught it.

'Yes. I'm very serious, Martin. I want you to listen carefully to what I'm going to say. For your own sake.'

'Go on, then. I'm listening.'

'Very well. So. You've conducted the whole business very well indeed. Like a well-planned military operation, one might say. With close attention to detail. But you're not out of the woods yet.'

'Aren't I?'

'No. I'm almost sure that the police have, ah, bought the suicide story. However, they will, inevitably and probably very soon, make certain discoveries that will make them highly suspicious.'

A cold twist of fear. *Ah*, Martin thought, *here it comes*.

He said, 'What discoveries?'

'I'm not going to tell you.'

'Why not?'

'Because it is vitally important that you do not know. That they surprise you.'

'I don't understand.'

'No. And that's a phrase that may well guarantee your safety.'

'My safety? What do you mean? I fucking *killed* you.'

'Yes, and I'm not ungrateful. Unlike my wife, I lacked the determination to do it myself. I wasted years, living.'

Some time passed. Inexplicably, Martin found himself crying again. 'Where are you, sir? When you're not here?'

'Nowhere, Martin. Not where you put me, if that's what's troubling you. The only place I am is my favourite place. Here. In the car. With you.'

'Oh, Jesus.'

'It's easier for me than it is for you. I understand that. But I'm not persecuting you. I'm not haunting you.'

'Yes you are! That's *exactly* what you're doing!'

'No. I'm protecting you.'

'*Protecting* me? You're driving me insane.'

He heard Godley shift in his seat. Then that same touch on his shoulder. Warm, feathery, like the belly of a bird settling there. This time he didn't shrink from it. After a long moment it withdrew.

Godley resumed. 'The police will come to the house again. They'll want to talk to you and Annie again.'

'Will they? Why?'

'For reasons I cannot divulge. But when they do, it is essential, Martin, *essential* that their attention is directed to the bureau in my study.'

'Why, sir?'

'Never mind. The bureau is locked. I would be reluctant to have it forced. It belonged to my father. The keys are in the little drawer set into the base of the carriage clock on the mantelpiece. Tell Annie that, Martin. Tell her to give them to the police when they ask. She'll be reluctant, but she must. Understand?'

'No.'

'Good. One last thing. On no account must you – or Annie, for that matter – open the bureau before the police return. Promise me that you won't, Martin.'

'I promise.'

A flight of ducks passed low overhead then landed, yakking, on the water.

'All will be well, Martin, all will be well. Now, what say we drive home via the A30? Let's open the old girl up a bit.'

PART FOUR

Close Attention
to Detail

May 1948

1

THE BAR OF THE WHITE HART began to fill with beery, cheerfully argumentative men wearing football scarves. Sheepstone and Panter carried their pints through into the lounge and sat at the small table close to the window. The inspector gazed out of it, sipped his bitter.

'Penny for them, sir?'

'Oh, nothing, really. Just what Archie would call an itch in the head.'

'Try me,' Panter said.

'How far is it, would you say, from Exmouth

railway station to where Godley's clothes were found? Three-quarters of a mile?'

'Something like that, yes.'

'That's quite a trek for an eighty-year-old in poor health, isn't it? One who has to be helped onto a train?'

'I suppose it is.'

'Simon Bloom told me – and this is between you, me and the gatepost, Ray – that Godley had more than enough pills to top himself if he'd wanted to. So why go to all that trouble, make up a tale about going to his solicitors, catching a train to Exmouth and chucking yourself in the sea, when you could do the job in the comfort of your own bed?'

Panter pulled the corners of his mouth down and shrugged. 'Who knows, sir. Balance of the mind disturbed.'

'Maybe. But both Martin Heath and Annie Luscombe stated that he seemed his usual self.'

'Yeah. But it's possible for someone to go nuts without it showing. On the outside, like. There's also the fact that his wife drowned herself.'

'So he did the same? What, to *join her* or some such nonsense?'

'I was thinking more along the lines of following her example, sir.'

Sheepstone humphed sceptically. He drank, then swirled his beer in his glass. 'Fancy topping these up, Ray?'

Panter glanced at his watch.

'Oh, come on, lad,' Sheepstone said. 'You can always blame me.'

'I usually do, sir.'

When Panter came back with the drinks Sheepstone said, 'What d'you make of those two, an'way? Heath and the lassie?'

'He's a bit of puzzle, sir, to my way of thinking. Educated type. Well spoken. Not your usual driver cum odd-job man.'

'That's what I thought. Could he be hiding anything, do you think? He struck me as being a bit . . . twitchy.'

'Annie, Miss Luscombe, did say that he'd had a bit of a time of it in the war. That it'd shaken him up.'

'Which means,' Sheepstone said, 'that he talks to her. About himself.'

Panter put his glass down precisely on the beer mat. 'What are you saying, sir?'

'Nothing. What d'you make of her?'

'Well, um, not the sharpest knife in the box. Very upset about Godley's disappearance, but . . .'

'But?'

'Well, maybe more concerned about herself than him. If the poor old bugger's dead, what's she going to do? She'd be out of a job. And a home.'

'Good-looking piece, though, wouldn't you say? Notice that, did you?'

Panter took a swig from his glass.

Sheepstone smiled and said, raising an eyebrow, 'I noticed you noticing that, Raymond.'

'Marriage hasn't affected my eyesight, sir,' Panter said, straight-faced. He glanced at his watch again.

'All right,' Sheepstone sighed. 'I'll let you go. So, Monday, unless anything crops up, get Martin Heath to come to the station and make a statement.'

'Sir.'

'Oh, and remind me to call whatsisname, Browning, first thing. We need to find out about Godley's next of kin.'

Annie Luscombe lowered herself onto her side, breathing in slow gasps, and pulled the bedclothes up to her waist. She ran her right hand down Martin Heath's chest and belly.

'Well,' she said, 'that was better. Last night you couldn't come off no matter what I did.'

'I know. I'm sorry. I was a bit . . . edgy.'

'No apology needed. You've more'n made up for it. But you're all right?'

'Yes, very.'

'Sure? You're not going to go funny on me, are you?'

He kissed her shoulder. 'No. Promise.'

'Good.'

She rolled away from him to pick up their wine glasses from the floor. He rejoiced in the wondrous curve of her back in the lamplight, the little dimples just above where her spine tucked itself between her buttocks. The miracle of her nakedness. And his own, so close to hers. She was the first woman he'd had sex with who knew his name and spoke his language. The first he hadn't paid with cash or food or mercy. And she was beautiful. And fearless.

She handed him his glass and leaned back on the pillows. Despite the fire in the grate the housekeeper's room was chilly but she didn't cover herself. She was proud of her breasts and liked the effect they had upon Martin. And the effect he had upon them.

2

SHEEPSTONE'S TELEPHONE rang at three minutes to nine.

'Yes, speaking. Ah, Mr Browning. I was just about to call you, as a matter of— Yes, that's correct. No, I'm afraid not.'

Ray Panter knocked and entered the room. Sheepstone mouthed the word 'Browning' at him and gestured him to sit.

'I see. And this is not something you're willing to discuss over the phone? Of course. Shall we say eleven o'clock? Good. Thank you for calling.'

He put the phone on its cradle.

'Bloody lawyers,' he said. 'Did you call Burra Hall yet?'

'Just about to, sir.'

'Don't bother. We've been summonsed to Exeter.'

Jonathan Browning's tall Georgian window commanded a fine view over the bombsite that until May 1942 had been Bedford Circus. The Luftwaffe had provided Browning with an uninterrupted sightline to the cathedral's Norman towers, from which he now turned away.

'And you are sure it was suicide?'

'All the evidence points that way, sir.'

'I must say I find it extremely surprising, as well as distressing. I've known Harold Godley for the better part of thirty years. I would not have thought him capable of such a desperate act.'

Panter said, 'When did you last see him, Mr Browning?'

'Ah. Precisely what I wanted to talk to you about. Please sit down, gentlemen.' Browning sat at his desk and made a steeple of his fingers.

The detectives settled themselves and waited.

'Harold came to see me in February. The twenty-fourth, to be precise. He instructed me to make changes to his will.'

He paused to rearrange his fingers. Sheepstone and Panter exchanged glances.

'Harold was rather unusual in that he had, in effect, no next of kin. His only son was killed in France in 1918. His wife, ah, predeceased him by many years. Harold's younger brother, Gerald, died in rather mysterious circumstances in Kenya in 1932. He was unmarried. Over the years, I have traced relatives on the, shall we say, more remote branches of the Godley family tree, but Harold felt no particular connection to them.'

Sheepstone leaned forward as if to speak but Browning held up a hand to silence him. Panter winced.

'Harold was a very wealthy man,' Browning continued.

'Is,' Sheepstone said.

'I beg your pardon, Inspector?'

'We have no body. As things stand, we are working on a presumption of death. Strictly speaking, your client is only missing.'

'Quite so, Inspector. I was coming to that.'

Sheepstone lifted a hand. 'Of course. I apologise. Merely a technicality. You were saying, sir?'

Browning huffily regathered himself. 'At a conservative estimate, his estate is currently valued at a shade under a million pounds.'

Fuck me, Panter thought and very nearly said.

'Harold was greatly preoccupied by the lack of an heir, or heirs. Over the years, he revised his will several times. Prior to our last meeting, the proceeds from his estate were to be divided among a number of charitable institutions. The British Legion was the main beneficiary. There were also generous cash bequests to his employees, both past and present.'

Panter glanced at his boss. Sheepstone's face was fixed and expressionless, a sure sign of impatience.

'That was how things stood until February, when Harold made changes that greatly surprised me, to put it mildly. Disturbed me, in fact.'

'Explain, please, Mr Browning.'

'According to the terms of his present will, the bulk of his estate goes to charity, as before. But a full quarter, including Burra Hall and its contents – and his Rolls-Royce, which is mentioned specifically – is left to Martin Heath.' Browning paused expectantly. He leaned back in his chair.

'Oh dear,' Sheepstone said quietly.

'Indeed. I was not happy about it. I strongly urged

Harold to reconsider. I mean, the fellow had been in Harold's employ for a mere nine months or so. But he was adamant.'

'Did he, Mr Godley, explain why he'd come to this decision?'

Browning sighed a long breath. 'Harold said that Heath had served his country bravely and well. That much would seem to be true, by the way. He was awarded the DCM in 1943. Did you know that?'

'No, we didn't.'

'Harold was also of the opinion that Heath had been severely damaged by the war. Psychologically. *Spiritually* was the word he used, actually. That he deserved to be looked after.'

'A quarter of a million is a heck of a lot of looking after,' Sheepstone said.

'Yes. Harold also said that Heath reminded him of his late son. Julian. In what respect, he didn't say.'

Sheepstone fell silent. To Panter's eye, he looked depressed.

'May I ask the obvious question, sir?'

'Yes, Ray, go ahead.'

'Mr Browning, do you think Martin Heath might have known he stood to come into a fortune in the event of Mr Godley's death?'

Browning spread his hands. 'Might Harold have told him? I've asked myself that, as you can imagine. Knowing Harold as I do, I'd think it highly unlikely. He was, is, a very private man. One might almost say secretive.'

'He might have been looking for a spot of gratitude.'

'I doubt it, Sergeant. Completely out of character.'

Sheepstone had been studying the carpet. Now he looked up. 'Did Mr Godley have a copy of the will in his possession, sir?'

'Yes, he did, Inspector. And you would be able to tell at once if it had been interfered with. The envelope was fastened with a red wax seal embossed with this firm's name. An old-fashioned touch that Harold insisted upon.'

Browning consulted his pocket watch and returned it to his waistcoat.

'Now then, gentlemen, I must leave you in ten minutes, so allow me to outline briefly the legal situation. As you quite properly observed, Inspector, Harold Godley is, technically, at this stage, missing, only presumed dead. The evidence, as you presented it to me, points to suicide but we have no proof positive of his death until the poor man's body is discovered. Which, from what you say, it may not be. In such cases, the missing person's will would not normally be executed for a period of seven years from the date of the disappearance. However, during that time the beneficiaries may apply to the court for the will to be enacted.'

Browning paused for dramatic effect.

'And I'm afraid that in this case they could well be successful.'

'Why so?'

'For three reasons. First, Harold was, in my considered opinion, of sound mind at the time when he instructed me. Second, given the weight of the circumstantial evidence and his continued disappearance, the court might very reasonably come to the conclusion that Harold did indeed end his own life. And third, there is no one, to the best of my knowledge, who might have grounds to contest the will.'

'I see,' Sheepstone said. 'So quite soon our lucky and gallant Mr Heath could find himself very well off indeed.'

'Yes, he could, Inspector. Unless . . .' Browning left the word dangling.

'Yes,' Sheepstone said. 'Unless.'

Outside, on the buckled pavement, in light rain, Sheepstone put his hat on, stuffed his hands in his pockets and said, 'Shit.'

Panter could not tell if his superior was referring to the German razing of the city's heart, the implications of the interview with Browning, or the solicitor himself. All three, possibly. He waited.

Sheepstone said, 'I could eat a dead horse between two mattresses. Is that half-decent place on Cathedral Green still standing, do you know?'

'I think so, sir. Don't know if they do horse, though.'

'Never mind. Lead me there, Ray. I can't think on an empty stomach.'

3

AT TWO O'CLOCK Martin drove Peg Maunder home in the van. She cried without the restraint she'd exercised in Annie's presence when she'd heard the news.

'Whyever would he do such a thing, Martin?'

'I don't know, Peg.'

'He was unhappy, course he was. But I never thought.'

'No.'

'Not a word nor sign, far as I could tell.'

'No.'

She dabbed at her eyes with her sleeve. 'I can't help

thinkin about his poor wife. How she went the same way.'

'What do you mean, Peg?'

'Drownded herself.'

'Did she?'

'Yes. Not long afore I took up my position. Threw herself into the reservoy. They say she couldn get over the death of her boy. Julian.'

'I didn't know that,' Martin said.

Peg Maunder sobbed quietly for a while then said, 'I don' know what's to become of us, Martin.'

'Nor do I. All we can do is carry on as normal and see what happens. It might be all right.'

'I don' even know if I should carry on comin up to the house.'

He said, 'I suppose that's up to you, Peg. I love your cooking, you know I do, but . . .'

'But the straight up and down of it is, without Mr Godley I haven' got a paid job no more.'

He brought the Morris to a halt at her cottage door. 'That's true,' he said.

'Bogger,' Peg said passionately.

Martin said, 'Listen. Why don't you take a day or two to think about it? I know Lily needs you. Annie and I can manage.'

She gripped his wrist. 'Two old maids, Martin, with nuthin comin in. We'd have to go on the parish. An I couldn' bear it. She's my sister but she drives me up the wall. Comin up to the house an' doin for Mr Godley's what's kep me sane as well as fed. I don' know what to do.'

'Peg.'

'T'aint your fault, Martin, bless you. You're in the same pickle as me. I shouldn go on about myself.'

He untied the cord that held the van's back doors closed and lugged out her heavy bicycle. The rain was coming down harder now. Peg stood on tiptoe and kissed him on the cheek.

Crossing the courtyard, Martin hesitated at the door to the stable block. It was possible, now that all things were possible, that Not-Dead Godley had thoughts about his cook's predicament. But no. He didn't want to talk to Godley. Not now.

Annie was waiting for him in the kitchen, leaning on the rail of the range, warming herself.

'Let's go to bed,' she said.

Her shocking directness thrilled him, as it had from the beginning.

But he shook his head. 'No, we mustn't.'

'Why not? We can do it whenever we like now.' She came to him, pressed herself against him. 'Come on. I really want to.'

'So do I.'

'I know.' She ran her hand down him. 'It's obvious. Let's go upstairs.'

'Annie. We can't. The police might turn up.'

'So what? Fucking's not against the law, as far as I know.'

'Annie.'

She relented a little. 'Do you think they'll come today?'

'They might.'

She sighed tragi-comically then backed herself against the table, pulling him with her. 'All right, then. I'll settle for a quickie. Here. On the table.'

'Jesus, Annie.'

She hurried at his buttons. Took him in hand. Smiled up at him. 'What a brazen hussy you've made of me, Mr Heath.'

4

SERGEANT BULLER SHOWED Martin into the interview room.

'If you'd sit there, sir? That's it. Now, Inspector Sheepstone will be joining us in a few minutes, so can I get you a cup of tea while we're waiting?'

'Um, yes. Thanks.'

The room was utterly inhospitable. The edge of the table was chipped. Martin ran his fingers along it then held them out and steadied them.

Buller returned with a clipboard under an arm and tea in a cup with a saucer, which he set down on the table.

He sat opposite Martin and took two freshly sharpened pencils from the breast pocket of his tunic. He checked his watch then busied himself writing along the dotted lines at the head of the statement form.

'Your middle name, Mr Heath?'

'John.'

'Date of birth?'

'October the twelfth, 1920.'

The door opened and Sheepstone and another man came in.

'Ah, Mr Heath. Thank you for coming.' He shook Martin's hand. 'This is Chief Inspector Reeve of the City of Exeter Police.'

'How do you do, Mr Heath.' Reeve was a slightly-built man with thinning hair Brylcreemed to his skull. There was something resentful about his bearing, as if he already found the occasion tedious. He too shook Martin's hand, then retreated to the corner near the door. He smothered a yawn before folding his arms and leaning against the wall.

Sheepstone sat on a chair a few feet from the table.

He said, 'As Sergeant Buller has no doubt explained, we need a formal statement from you for our files. Just the facts relating to the day of Mr Godley's disappearance. We'd be very grateful if you could recall any details in addition to what you have already told us. Sergeant Buller will write down what you say, then ask you to read it through. If you are satisfied that it's accurate, sign it and then we're done. Is that all right?'

'Yes,' Martin said. He lowered his cup onto the saucer using both hands.

'Good,' Sheepstone said, leaning back and crossing his legs. 'Over to you, then, Sergeant.'

In the kitchen of Burra Hall, Annie was fully aware of DS Panter's gaze on her as she made a pot of tea. It was as real as fingers. She put the pot on the table next to the milk jug and the sugar bowl and the little dish for the tea strainer. Keeping up standards. Not letting things slide.

Panter said, 'What d'you think you'll do, Annie?'

'How d'you mean?'

'You know. I mean, with Mr Godley dead.'

'You don' know that,' she said fiercely. 'He might not be. He might turn up.'

'True. But I don't think it's likely, do you?'

She turned her face heroically into the light from the window. 'I'll stay here till I'm turned out. Someone've got to keep the place up. It'd be a sin to let it go to wreck and ruin.'

'Yes, it would. I was thinking more about you your-self. How you'd live. It's none of my business, but—'

'I've got a bit put away. It's not like there's much to spend your wages on, is there?' She poured the tea. 'D'you take sugar?'

'Yes. Thanks.' Panter took a packet of Senior Service from his pocket. 'Smoke?'

'We're not allowed, normally. But yeah. Just this once. Thanks.' She leaned into his flame.

He said, 'What about Martin?'

'What about him?'

'Well, he's out of a job too, isn't he? Has he said anything about what he's going to do?'

'No,' Annie said contemptuously. 'Since Mr Godley went missin, all he does is mess about with that fuckin car.'

Panter blinked at the obscenity. He lowered his cup. 'What do you think of him, Annie?'

'What, Martin? He's all right, I s'pose. A bit stuck up. A bit on the posh side. Keeps himself to himself, mostly. He has trouble with his nerves because of the war and that.'

'Yes, you told me that before.'

'Did I?'

'So he talked to you about the war, did he?'

Annie blew smoke. 'No.'

'But you knew he'd had a rough time.'

'Only cause Mr Godley told me so. Soon after he come here, Mr Godley says to me, *Annie, be nice to Mister Heath. He've been through the mill.*'

'And are you nice to him, Annie? Do you get along?'

She tapped ash into the dish of tea leaves. 'Not in the way you're thinking,' she said.

Sergeant Buller's handwriting was surprisingly elegant. His spelling was faultless, his punctuation less so.

Sheepstone said, 'Anything you want to change or add, Martin?'

Martin looked up from the paper. 'No. That's it, I think.'

'Thank you, sir,' Buller said. 'If you would sign your name just here?'

Martin did so and looked up. Sheepstone remained in his seat, legs crossed. Reeve, in the corner, was examining his fingernails. Buller leaned back and crossed his arms, smiling pleasantly.

Sheepstone said, 'There's one tiny detail bothering me, Martin. An eyewitness who saw Mr Godley in Exmouth at approximately four fifteen on the day he disappeared states that he was carrying a bag of some sort. But on neither of the occasions we've spoken to you have you mentioned it.'

'No, I . . . Yes, he had his briefcase with him. I forgot. I'm sorry. Is it important?'

'I don't know. It might be. Can you describe it to me?'

'Um, old, black. Just a briefcase.'

'Any idea what might have been in it?'

'No. Papers, I suppose. He was going to see his solicitor.'

'Yes, of course. It's a bit odd, though, that it hasn't been found, don't you think? It wasn't with his other belongings on the beach. And it hasn't been located in the Lost Property office at St David's, which is where it would end up if he'd left it on a train.'

Martin said, 'I don't know what you want me to say. I can't explain it. I'm sorry I forgot to mention it. Do you want me to change my statement?'

'Oh no,' Sheepstone said. 'No need for that. Like I said, just a detail.'

'So can I go now?'

'Yes, of course. Sergeant Buller will drive you back whenever you like. But before you go, Martin, I wonder if you'd mind helping us to get a better picture of Mr Godley. His state of mind and so forth.'

'What do you mean?'

'Well, you spent time with him.'

'Not a lot, actually. Mostly when I was driving him.'

'And you talked at such times?'

'Yes. When he felt like it.'

'Of course. What did you talk about?'

'Um . . . this and that. The car, things that needed doing round the house. The weather. That sort of thing.'

'Nothing more, shall we say, personal? Revealing? About himself?'

Martin shook his head. 'No. He wasn't like that.' He hesitated. 'He talked about his son once or twice. Julian. He was killed in 1918.'

'Yes,' Sheepstone said. 'Was this recently that Mr Godley spoke about him?'

'Fairly recently, yes.'

'Hmm. Do you think it might have been preying on his mind?'

'I honestly couldn't say. Perhaps.'

Sheepstone nodded, looking down at the scuffed brown linoleum.

Martin cleared his throat and said, 'Inspector, I . . .'

Sheepstone looked up. 'And did you talk to Mr Godley about your war, Martin?'

'I . . . I might have.'

'I have to confess that until a couple of days ago we had no idea that you had such a distinguished military record. We were very impressed, weren't we, Archie?'

Buller's face was all genial approbation. 'We were, sir. Very.'

Martin's hands started to go. He clasped them together on the table and stared at them.

Sheepstone, concerned, said, 'I'm sorry, Martin. Is this something you prefer not to talk about?'

'Yes.'

'I can understand that. But you talked about it to Mr Godley.'

'He's my employer. He asked me.'

'Of course. Is that why you took the job down here, by the way? To get away from it all? A bit of peace and quiet? Or peace of mind?'

'Something like that, yes.'

'And has it worked, would you say?'

Martin made himself look up. All three policemen were watching him keenly now.

'Yes. I'm fine. Thank you.'

Reeve, his silence, worried him. He caught the man's eye. Reeve pursed his lips into a sort of smile and nodded slightly. As if to say, *I know what you've been through. You're doing all right.*

5

DS PANTER FINISHED his second cup of tea and said, 'One of the problems we have is that we don't know much about Mr Godley. I mean, apart from Martin's description we don't even know what he looks like. Are you sure there aren't any photographs?'

'Not that I know of.'

'That's a bit strange, don't you think?'

Annie shrugged. 'Not really. I haven't had my picture took since I was at school. Have you?'

'Um. Well, yes. Wedding photographs, and so on.'

'Oh,' Annie said, sounding ever so slightly disappointed. 'You're married, are you?'

'Yes. Expecting our first child in September, as a matter of fact.'

'Congratulations.'

'Thank you.' He blinked away an image of her backed against the table, her skirt hoisted over her hips. He said, 'So tell me about him, Annie. Mr Godley. What was he like?'

'What, to work for?'

'Yeah. And in general.'

'Well, he was kind, in a quiet sort of a way. He treated me nice, never no trouble. Except when he got taken bad. That used to put the wind up me, what with us being so far from help.'

'He was an invalid?'

'Oh no. Just old and poorly. And sad.'

'Depressed, do you mean?'

She shrugged again. 'Maybe. I dunno what that means, really. Just a very sad old gentleman.'

'Can't have been much fun,' Panter suggested. 'For you, I mean.'

'You just get on with it, don't you? Anyhow, he was cheerful enough when he talked to you. It's just when you caught him unawares, as you might say, he looked like . . . No. I mustn't say that.'

'Go on, Annie. Please. I need all the help I can get here. He looked like . . . ?'

It seemed that she might cry. 'God forgive me,' she said, 'I was goin to say he looked like someone waitin to die.'

Sheepstone glanced at his watch.

'One last question, Martin. It's a bit of a strange one, but did you *like* Mr Godley?'

'Um . . . he was a very decent employer. Is.'

'I'm sure he was. But that's not quite what I asked you. I was wondering what your personal feelings towards him were.'

'Well . . . I liked him, yes.' He looked at his clasped hands again. 'I'm sorry. That's not really true. I just felt very sorry for him. And he worried me.'

'May I ask why?'

Martin took a deep breath and gasped it out. 'He was so bloody *sad*. And . . . and frail. And *cut off*. Do you know what? I've worked for him for nearly a year now, and in all that time he's not had a single visitor. Unless you count the doctor. I used to think, *Dear God, don't let me live that long if that's how you end up.*'

'Yes, indeed. I couldn't agree more.' Sheepstone

studied the lino again, as if the demarcations of his own mortality were recorded on it. Then he looked up, brightened a little. 'As you say, a very lonely man. But not alone. He had Mrs Maunder and Miss Luscombe. And you, of course. He was clearly very fond of you.'

Martin, frowning, said, 'Why do you say that?'

'Well, considering that, as you say, you've only been with Mr Godley for less than a year, you'd obviously become quite close.'

Martin felt the worm of fear hibernating in his heart stir. 'I wouldn't say that. What gave you that idea?' His eyes swivelled between the three policemen. They hadn't moved but seemed closer to him somehow. 'Is that what Annie told you?'

'No,' Sheepstone said. 'No. We just assumed that, well, your relationship with Mr Godley was rather more than just employer and employee. That perhaps he had paternal feelings toward you.'

The worm lifted its head. Martin's left leg jittered. 'What on earth makes you say that?'

'Well,' Sheepstone said, 'apart from anything else, the fact that he made you a beneficiary of his will.'

'What?'

'That he left you an amount of money. Quite a generous amount, as it happens.'

The worm rose thick into his throat. He struggled to speak. 'Did he?'

'Yes. Would you like to know how much?'

'I . . . I suppose so.'

'A little over a hundred and eighty thousand pounds,' Sheepstone said levelly. 'In cash and bonds. Plus Burra Hall. Oh, and the Rolls.'

Shock lengthened into silence. The worm became a noose. The trap door beneath him creaked. Reeve wore a hangman's sorrowful face. *Oh, Jesus.*

'No. That's not . . . That can't be true. It's some sort of mistake.'

'No, Martin. There's no mistake. I've spoken to Mr Godley's solicitor. The one he did not, in fact, have an appointment with on Wednesday.'

'I don't understand. I couldn't . . . He . . .'

'You're a rich young man, Martin. Unless, of course, Mr Godley is still alive. But I think we both know he's not, don't we?'

Martin fumbled for his cigarettes, but his hands couldn't manage the packet. It fell onto the table. He leaned forward on his elbows and covered his face with his hands.

*

DS Panter said, 'So what did he do? How did he spend his time?'

'What d'you mean?'

'Well, you know. What's an average day in the life of Burra Hall like?'

Annie humphed an amused little sound. It seemed to Panter intimate. He pushed his Senior Service across the table.

She shook her head. 'No, ta. Well, I get up at half six and get that moody bugger goin.' She aimed a thumb at the range. 'Half seven, I take him his breakfast up, along with hot water for his shave and that. Put his clothes out and so on. He'll come down about half eight. Then if the weather aint too bad he'll go outside for a stroll about. Maybe have a word with Mr. Gates about the garden and such.'

'He was all right on his legs then, was he?'

'Oh, yes. He liked a bit of a walk. He used that stick, but he didn' need to, you ask me. He mostly used it to point at things with.'

'Right.'

'Then Auntie Peg, Mrs Maunder, comes in about ten. Sets about makin lunch, then the dinner for later. Mr Godley liked to be in here with her. He'd sit where you are. He liked listenin to Peg's gossip.'

Panter said, 'And where would Martin be, all this time?'

'I dunno. Doin this and that.' Annie leaned back in her chair and levelled a look at him. 'We keep comin back to Mr Martin bloody Heath, don't we? D'you know somethin about him I don't?'

'No. I'm just, like I say, trying to get the full picture.'

She hummed sceptically, but resumed. 'So, we'd have lunch . . .'

'Together?'

'Oh, no,' Annie said, as if the idea was rather shocking. 'Mr Godley took his meals in the dining room. Me and Peg – and Martin, sometimes, to save you askin – had ours in here. Then he'd – Mr Godley, that is – have a little nap on the day bed in his study. A couple of times a week Martin'd take him out in the Rolls. He did love that. He loved that car.' She seemed on the verge of tears again. She sniffed, lengthily.

'Where did they go, Annie? Do you know?'

'Just here and there, I think. Not very far, on account of how it drinks petrol. A gas-guzzler, Martin calls it.'

'Yes,' Panter said. 'I dare say it is. What about the evenings?'

Annie puffed her cheeks out and expelled air. *Pewf.* It made Panter smile.

'What?'

'Evnins,' she said. 'That's when I don't know what to do with myself. Can I change my mind about that fag?'

'Help yourself,' he said.

He lit her up. She inhaled, blew out a plume of smoke. Picked a fleck of tobacco from her lower lip.

'Just out of interest,' he said, 'when'd you last have a night out?'

'Why? Are you offerin?'

'I don't think Irene would approve.'

'The wife.'

'Yes,' he said.

She looked steadily at him for a second or two before she tapped ash into the dish. She said, 'After dinner Mr Godley usually goes back into his study. He've got the wireless in there and sometimes he'll listen to that. Or read the paper. Or write in his journal. Then—'

Panter interrupted her. 'Journal? What, like a diary?'

'I dunno. His journal is what he called it.'

'That's interesting, Annie. Where'd he keep it, do you know?'

'In his bureau.'

She gave the word a posh inflection, as if she were proud of it.

*

Sheepstone stood up and went to Martin and put a hand on his shoulder. 'We'll leave you alone for a couple of minutes, Martin. This has obviously come as something of a shock. I'll get someone to bring you another cup of tea. All right?'

Martin took his hands from his face and put them flat on the table. He didn't raise his head. He said, 'I didn't know. I don't understand it. He never said anything.'

Sheepstone said, 'Sugar?'

Martin nodded. 'Please.'

When he looked up he was alone in the room. He groped for his lighter.

Reeve and Buller were waiting in Sheepstone's office. Sheepstone closed the door behind him and said, 'Well, John?'

Reeve said, 'If he knew, he's the best fucking actor I've ever seen. Knocks Charles Laughton into a cocked hat.'

'Archie?'

'I agree, sir. He went white as a sheet. I don't know as you could fake that.'

'I thought he might actually pass out on the spot,' Reeve said, dryly amused.

'Yes,' Sheepstone said. 'But the question is *why*?

Because he was genuinely shocked? Or because he realised we'd found a motive?'

'For murder, Ivan? I still can't see it. The evidence for suicide is pretty damn conclusive, if you ask me, body or no body. I've met some bloody good liars in my time but I'd bet my house on Heath not knowing about Godley's will. In which case . . .'

'I know,' Sheepstone said and stuffed his hands into his pockets. 'Damn it.'

'It was worth a try, though,' Reeve said.

'Yep, I suppose so.' The detective inspector sighed. 'I don't know, John. There's a smell comes off this one. I can't get it out of my nostrils.'

The phone rang.

'Yes? Hello, Ray.'

Sheepstone listened without speaking for a whole minute then said, 'All right. Aye, bring them in. What? For God's sake, Ray. It's none of her business. Tell her we'll do her for withholding evidence if you have to. No. Inconclusive, I'd say. Yeah. Bye.'

He lowered the hand piece onto the cradle and gazed at it for a moment as if it were a disappointing grandchild.

He said, 'You might as well take Mr Heath home, Archie.'

6

22nd of April 1892

I am a father! Eleanor was
delivered of a son shortly
after 2 o'clock this afternoon.
Her labour was long and hard
— her cries were clearly audible
downstairs — the whole house—

~hold in a state of nerves. I must have smoked five cigars. The birth itself however, was not diofficult. This according to the midwife, (although I might venture a different opinion) She is much recovered now (9pm) and a little ealier this evening enjoyed a few sips of champagne by way of celebration.

Julian is a dear little thing with quite a lot of dark hair and a yellow nose. Dr Harwood assures me that this is quite normal. He pronounced Julian to be sound, strong

*and well formed. Thank God!
Now I shall have to brace
myself for the inevitable visit
of E's mother and*

The light in the flat diminished suddenly; at the same instant rain flurried against the window. Sheepstone reached up and switched on the standard lamp beside his armchair. He added another inch of Johnnie Walker to his glass.

Clearly, the birth of his son had prompted Harold Godley to embark upon his journal. The handwriting was bold, cursive, pleased with itself. It was the first entry in the first of the fourteen volumes heaped on the low table alongside Sheepstone's chair. Of these, twelve were quarto-sized hard-covered notebooks with marbled endpapers. Two – the final two, covering the years 1940 to the present – were cheaper affairs: coarser and thinner paper into which the ink had sometimes leached, between indigo cardboard covers. In these, the now withered writing had set off across the page at unpredictable angles, often coming to a halt midsentence. The volumes were labelled I to XIV.

*

Ray Panter had returned to the station and lugged the books up to Sheepstone's office.

'They took up both the lower drawers in the desk,' Panter said. 'This is the one – excuse me, sir – you'd be interested in, I think. I reckon the last entry was written just before he disappeared. It's a bit difficult to read.' He took one of the blue-bound books from the top of the pile, licked his forefinger and turned the pages back.

Sheepstone and Reeve leaned down, frowning, deciphering.

Ten minutes later Reeve straightened up, grimacing, his hand on the small of his back. 'That does it for me, Ivan. Not exactly a suicide note, I grant you. But good as. I'd say we can put this one to bed.'

Sheepstone had been forced to agree. But, later, he'd got Panter to give him a lift home and help him carry Godley's journal up to the flat. He'd made a late lunch – a corned beef sandwich with pickled onions – then settled himself in his armchair and begun to skim through the dead man's life. A life, it gradually emerged, that had promised to be a walk through a pleasant meadow; but the meadow had been strewn with tripwires and mines.

Technically, of course, it wasn't a journal. The entries were continuous on the page, but chronologically sporadic, their dates often separated by months, even years. At first, Godley had written a few sentences almost every day, recording the minutiae of Julian's development, anxieties over his and his mother's health, and so forth. After a year and a half, these obsessive observations became admixed with other matters that had equal or greater claim on his attention. By 1900, references to *J* had become intermittent and, more often than not, anxious. Nor did Julian feature frequently in Volume VI and the first part of Volume VII, covering the years 1914 to 1918, despite the fact that Godley must have lived in a continuous state of dread; his son had joined the Oxfordshire and Buckinghamshire Light Infantry and gone to war just two months after graduating from Magdalen.

One entry had caught Sheepstone's eye:

12th of June 1918
J home on leave. Awfully changed. He seems 10 —more— years older. Distant. He's

dreadfully thin and his hands shake. He and I hiked to Belstone, glorious weather. He found it taxing. He'd caught a whiff of gas, as he put it. Lunch in the pub. Despite my best efforts, I could not engage him in meaningful conversation. I suggested that he report himself to the medical board but he became angry and I dropped the subject.

& beside herself with anxiety of course. Awkward moment at dinner when we noticed that she was crying. I flung down his cutlery and

retreated to his room.
I was angry with him, &
was angry with me.
Fairly awful.

But despite the calamities in France that threatened to deprive him of his son, Godley, in his journal, had restricted himself almost entirely – obsessively – to mundane and mostly domestic matters: his finances, the difficulty of finding able-bodied men for his tenanted farm or to maintain the house, problems with servants, vagaries of the weather. The written equivalent of a man whistling in the dark, Sheepstone thought.

And to no avail.

21st of Oct, 1918

My son is dead

Nothing further for eighteen months. Then, in unsteady writing:

22ⁿᵈ of April 1920

J's birthday
& in a dreadful state all
day. Inconsolable. Or at
least I cannot console her.
I do not know how to, nor if she
wants me to try. She has
not spoken more than a
dozen words to me all day —
or anyone else. She spent
the whole afternoon in J's
room. I heard her weeping
through the door. Could not
persuade her to come downstairs

despite several attempts.
She has procured a tailor's
mannequin from somewhere
and dressed it in G's best
uniform returned to us with
the rest of his things. Hideous.
I cannot bear to look at it. I
cannot go into that room now
10 o'clock. In the study drinking
whisky. House silent.
Julian
Julian
Julian
Ju

The next entry reached almost to the bottom of a left-hand page.

1st of May 1920

Haunted by some memory of this day back in Q, Victoria's time. Ma and Pa and Gerald. Gerald and I in white outfits many other children similarly attired dancing round a maypole, doing complicated things with ribbons. Getting mixed up, falling over. Very ashamed, but Pa laughing and applauding. Poor E hardly improved at all. Silent, withdrawn, unreachable.

*Then bouts of busying about
the house in a temper.
I found Mary sobbing on the
back stairs yesterday, and I
should not be surprised if
Cook were to pack her bags
shortly.
Summoned Laywood Wednes,
but I flatly refused to see
him
I really don't know what to do.*

The right-hand page had been ripped out. A thinning triangle of paper closest to the binding had survived. Of the date, *5th of Ma* had survived. Studying the letters on the rest of the remnant, Sheepstone came to the conclusion that Godley had scrawled *Eleanor* over and over again. Then torn her out.

It was at this point in his reading that Sheepstone

had gone to his kitchen for the bottle of whisky. He was himself a widower who had lost a child.

Godley had not resumed his journal until August 1922. The brief account of his pilgrimage to where his son had died was peculiarly flat, mechanically descriptive. The landscape was *'dreary, rather like parts of Lincolnshire'*. The *auberge* he'd stayed in was *'clumsily restored, the food ghastly'*. The only touch of bitterness was in his mention of the local agriculture *'going on as if nothing had happened'*.

This same emotionless, neurasthenic tone characterised the rest of the journal. Until the last volume, anyway. Unless his cars were mentioned. He'd perked up, then. He'd written a whole page about the Rolls-Royce Twenty he'd bought in 1926.

Who the hell were you, Harold Godley?

Sheepstone picked up the lapsed passport that Panter had also found in Godley's desk. It had been stamped only once, by the *Douane* in Calais on the nineteenth of August 1922. The photograph showed a middle-aged man wearing a stiff collar and a tie. Prominent forehead, receding hairline. Narrow face with high cheekbones, thin lips, deep lines between the wings of his nose and his jaw, eyes blanked by camera flash. A man already, a quarter of a century ago, on nodding terms with death.

Sheepstone, the son of a miner, had grown up in a cluster of low cottages on a wind-strimmed hillside. His family had shared an outdoor privy with their neighbours. He had acute memories of queuing for a shit in the cold hard rain. As that boy, the idea that the rich suffered tribulations would have been incomprehensible. As a man, the knowledge that they did had sometimes afforded him a certain satisfaction.

It did not do so now. He felt dismayed.

7

SHEEPSTONE WENT to the window and drew the curtains over his unwelcome reflection. The room was chill. He considered lighting a fire, but the messiness of the business and the poor quality of his coal deterred him. He fetched his dressing gown from the bedroom and wrapped himself in it. He returned to his chair, drank from his glass and reached for Godley's final volume. He brisked through it until Heath made his first appearance in the spring of last year.

23.ᵃᵈ of April 1947

Yesterday engaged the services
of MR Martin Heath.
Came highly reccommended
by young Jimmy Locke.
Impressive war record.
Personable young man.
Disturbing encounter though.
Same shellshock symptoms
as of on his last leave. Shakes,
etc. Awful moment when I
remembered it was J's birthday
(How could I have forgotten?)
Coincidence or something else?
Foolishness. Reminded me
of him. Showed him the

of him. Showed him the Phantom. He was agog: I almost laughed. Silly I suppose to employ an unstable person as a driver, but we have a debt to these young men. Annie a bit sulky but she'll get over it. Thinks she owns the place.

The next entry was dated 17th May, same year. It had been many years, Sheepstone had noted, since Godley had recorded anything during the earlier part of May.

Heath took me on a drive. Wanted to see how he handled the Phantom. Nervous but competent. Clearly loves the old girl, which is what matters.

> *And she likes, trusts him
> I think. Startled him using
> the speakerphone!
> He's very quiet.
> Like*

Like J? Was that what the old man had intended to write but veered away from the thought? If so, he couldn't stop himself returning to it, repeatedly and, in the end, obsessively. In August – by which time 'Heath' had modulated into 'Martin' then simply 'M' – Godley had written

> *This am, picked last of the
> raspberries. Returning
> through the yard saw M
> walking on the Phantom.
> In shirtsleeves, braces
> dangling. Took him for G.*

Quite sure it was him. May
have called out his name.
Awful moment. Felt dizzy
thought I might fall. Dropped
the punnet of fruit. It had
to help me into the house.
I hope I am not losing my mind.
Increasingly forgetful etc.
Natural I suppose. My age.
But let me not go mad.
Shameful
Talk to Bloom?

*But you did go mad, didn't you, you poor old sod?
Or something like it. Although you were too proud to
let it show.*

Sheepstone drained his glass, then poured another
measure while telling himself not to.

Had Godley lost his marbles before he'd changed
his will? Browning had judged him to be in his right

mind, despite having every reason and inclination for testifying otherwise. And Godley's brief account of that meeting almost nine months after taking Heath on was cogent enough.

... he was most reluctant. Spoke to me as if I were a wayward child. A good lawyer and a decent mom but a pompous b— I had to put my foot down very firmly. Anyway it is done. And shall stay done. A load off my mind. Cold and tired by the time I got home, but felt lighter somehow. Enjoyed my supper.

Thereafter, few entries. But they made for hard reading in more senses than one. Sheepstone recalled with displeasure Ray Panter licking his finger before turning the pages.

3rd of March, 1948

Bitter. Indoors all day
not at all well. Imagined
strange sounds in the house;
howling, rattling. J's voice.
Our last argument.
We parted on such bad terms.
Never put right.
M built up the fire in my
bedroom before I retired.
Good of him.
My son

14th

For some nights – and days –
– tormented by same dream
of E. Of E drowning
Falling down and down.
Wearing her wedding dress.
Also in the water with her
but she is below me and I
cannot quite reach her hand
to catch her, to stop her and then
she is disappearing into the
darkness below. I call and call
her name but no sound comes
from my mouth.
Or so I thought until last
night I awoke to find H
standing by the bed. Said

he wanted to wake me but thought it might be dangerous to do so. Misplaced kindness.

Worst thing is that in the dream I cannot see E's face. Obscured by her hair. And dear cruel God, what a terrible admission this is – in my waking hours I cannot ~~see her face~~. Cannot bring it to mind. I have ~~forgotten~~ what my dear beautiful wife looked like. How is such a thing possible?
How I regret destroying in my manic grief her photographs, burning her portrait. Fool!

Without memory, are we still human? I know in my sleep when this dream is coming but I cannot wake from it. It is past 10.30 but I am afraid of going to bed. The bitter time of year approaches. I don't know if I can face it yet again

Godley's underlinings had pierced the paper.

1st of April 1948

S brought my breakfast and when I tapped the boiled egg with the spoon it proved to be hollow. Mrs M has been

playing this April Fool's trick
on me for the better part of
20 years (A has the real egg
in her pocket). It always catches
me out because I forget what
day it is. But today for some
reason this harmless jest
threw me into a rage. I hurled
the tray from the bed. A shocked,
scolded me. And then I burst
into tears.

Like a child.
When SSS SH tells of something
that embarrassed or confounded
her, she says, "I didn't know
what to do with myself."
I don't know what to do with
myself. I live without purpose.

7th

The poet Eliot says that
April is the cruellest month.
(Heard him on the wireless the
other evening which is why
I thought of it I suppose)
Hope and all that renewal, etc.
Not when one is 84 and nothing
May is worse

9th of April

Beautiful weather for once
HH drove up onto the high moor
then on to Moretonhampstead.
The Phantom in fine fettle.
If only he knew. Made him
take tea with me in a cafe.

Coaxed a little more of his
war experience out of him.
Wrong of me perhaps. He's
modest and I know it disturbs
him but for some reason I
need to know. I would never
speak of it. Not to me. Or€
as far as I know. The sheer
contrariness of the young
being so familiar with death,
dealing it, dealing with it,
while a very old mom
while a very old mom lives
on, pointlessly.
Uselessly.
The dream again this p.m.
Bloom's potions not proof
against it.

22nd

A whole year since SH first
came here. Makes the date
less painful perhaps.
Was I harsh with you? Yes
a harsh father. Cannot forgive
myself and now no one left to
forgive me. I did not. For
sending you away to school.
Never the same between us after
that. You see I thought you
needed the companionship of
other boys of your own age.
You were a solitary child
and

No. Not true. No point lying to you—or myself now. Far too late. I thought you were too close to your mother. That you were growing up soft. Effeminate. So I again NO! Worse than that I was jealous. Envious. Both. I ~~resented~~ your closeness to her. So I sent you away. There, it is ~~said~~ at last.

A space on the page and a slight change in the handwriting suggested to Sheepstone that Godley had resumed the next day or later, although under the same date.

I was always wrong about you. When you were up at Oxford your mother and I came up to see you, do you remember? 1912, was it?

You and your friend – I
have forgotten his name –
took us on a punt and we
picnicked beneath a willow.
I thought

Your CO wrote – I have
it still somewhere
of your exemplary and
inspirational bravery.
You see? I remember.
I was always wrong about
you. I have been wrong
all my life. I wish I were
done with it.

We parted for the last time
with a handshake like
business acquaintances.
Still angry with each other

we should have embraced.
You embraced your mother
while I stood watching.
When did I last put my
arms around you, J?
Not since you were ~~a~~ small
boy I think.

Today ~~W~~ helped me out of
the Phantom and I wanted
to
You hated me didn't you?
Is that why you volunteered
for that last patrol? Hoping
intending, to die knowing
it would kill me too?
You succeeded. Over and
over again

189

29th

The awful dream again but different. I reached E's hand and she grasped it. Felt a sort of joy but understood that she didn't want me to pull her up, but wanted me to follow her down. Saw and remembered her lovely face. We went down into the greenish darkness together, but then in a kind of panic I forced her white fingers apart and struggled up towards the air while she faded away.

I awoke alone in my room,
the light behind the curtain,
and felt a bitter disappointment
that I was still alive.
Cowardice.
I shall be brave like you
E. Try me again.

The last entry was brief.

4th May

Enough, then.

Everything in place.

No more

Sheepstone closed the book and sat with it on his lap for some time. Then laughter from the street prompted him to look at his watch. Almost nine o'clock. He felt a sudden spasm of anxiety, or fear. He could not remain alone with Godley's ghost a moment longer. He put on his coat and hat and hurried to the pub, towards light and human voices.

8

SHORTLY AFTER TWO in the morning, Martin left the coach house via the tack room. The sky had cleared. A wash of moonlight glazed the wet cobbles of the courtyard. He re-entered the house by the scullery door and followed the weak beam of the electric torch up the main stairs.

Annie had been deeply asleep when he'd eased himself out of bed almost an hour earlier but now, despite his caution, she stirred.

'Martin?'

'Ssh. It's OK.'

'Where've you been?'

'Thought I heard a noise. I went to look around but I must have imagined it.'

'What time is it?'

'No idea. Go back to sleep. I'm sorry I woke you.'

He sat on the edge of the bed and removed his shoes. Then he was immobilised by the things whirling in his head. He felt the mattress shift, then Annie's warm hand running up his back.

'Martin? What's the matter?'

'Nothing. It's all right.'

'You sure? You're not . . .'

'No. I'm all right, honestly.'

'Get back into bed then, you daft sod.'

He laughed and turned to her. Her face was ghostily silvered by the faint light from the uncurtained window.

She tugged at his shirt. 'Come on.' She exaggerated a shudder when his body was against hers. 'Oof, you're freezing.'

'Sorry.'

She turned away from him and he shaped himself against her back. She took his hand and guided it to the soft heat between her legs. 'You're sure you're all right?'

194

'Yes,' he said. 'Everything's fine.'

'Good.'

'Annie?'

'Mmmn?'

'There's something I need to tell you.'

She shunted her rump against him. Pressed his fingers into her. 'Can it wait until the morning?'

Yes, he said, or thought, as his body began its slow rejoicing. *It can wait*.

PART FIVE

Wasp Weather

August 1948

1

AUGUST, AND ON A WHIM Martin brought the
Sunbeam Talbot to a stop at the Thatch in Cheriton
Bishop. The interview with Jonathan stuffed-shirt
Browning had been frigid – hostile, really – but perfectly satisfactory. From Martin's point of view, at
least. Browning reminded him of certain staff officers
he'd met during the war: pompous, jealous of their
own authority, but weak-kneed when faced by men
who knew what killing was about.

He carried his pint through to the pub's garden
where a few tables and chairs had been set up. None

were occupied. He settled himself and lit a cigarette. He opened the *Western Gazette* and turned to the Notice of Auction pages, in which he had an interest.

It was hot in the garden, but not pleasantly so. The sky was blank, the air thick and heavy. Wasp weather. Two of the little bastards took an interest in his beer; he blew smoke at them.

A shadow fell across his newspaper and he looked up.

'Hello, Martin.' Sheepstone had his hat in one hand and his jacket draped over his arm. The other hand held a pint glass. 'Busy? Or mind if I join you?'

Sheepstone sat, not waiting for a reply.

'I hate this time of year,' he said. 'Clammy. Can't get enough air.' He flapped his hand at a nuisance. 'And bloody wasps. And gnats. I was in church last Sunday and we sang *All things bright and beautiful, all creatures great and small, all things wise and wonderful, the Lord God made them all*. And I was thinking, what about bloody wasps and gnats?'

He sipped his beer.

'Or liver flukes. Or tapeworms. Or parasites in general. How are you doing, Martin?'

'OK, thanks.'

'The air is always better up on the moor, of course.

You'll have found that, no doubt. More of a breeze. Fresher.'

'Yes.'

Sheepstone drank again. He set his glass down, smacking his lips and frowning critically. 'Difficult weather for keeping beer decent too. I'd say they haven't quite succeeded, wouldn't you?'

'I don't know. It tastes all right to me. But then I'm not much of a beer drinker, as a rule.'

'No,' Sheepstone said. 'You'd be more of a wine man, eh?' He studied Martin amiably for a moment or two, then said, 'I know how you did it. Obvious, really. Godley never got on that train. He was already dead. But you turned up at the station in the Rolls, and someone got out of the back of it. Who else could it have been but Harold Godley? Who else gets out of the back of a Phantom at Okehampton and has his ticket bought for him by his chauffeur? Bolsover, the stationmaster, saw what he expected to see. Old Godley, all muffled up against the cold. Not that it was particularly chilly. But then he felt the cold more than most. According to you, anyway. And that's what was seen in Exmouth too. A well-dressed elderly gent, less than average height, hat, collar up, scarf up to his nose.'

Martin stubbed out his cigarette and resisted the urge to light another.

'It was risky, though. It was fairly unlikely that there'd be many, if any, other passengers travelling first-class between Okehampton and Exmouth on a Wednesday afternoon. But there was always that chance. That someone might have got into the same compartment. Someone who might want to strike up a conversation. What would she do then, Martin, I wonder? Keep her face covered and pretend she'd lost her voice? Hide behind the *Daily Telegraph*? It took some nerve, any road. And she got away with it. I almost admire her. You can tell her that, if you like.'

'Who are we talking about?'

Sheepstone took another sip of bitter. 'So she got to Exmouth without mishap and found her spot on the beach. Sat down, I expect. She wouldn't have been seen from the road because it's the other side of the dunes. She had her shoes and a skirt in the brief-case. And a headscarf perhaps? Yes, I think so. Oh, and a shopping bag or somesuch to put the trousers in. She changed her clothes and made a neat little pile of Godley's things. Put a stone in the hat to stop it blowing away. A slight mistake, that. It made my nose twitch. But you wanted it found, of course. Then she chucked the briefcase into the sea. Job done. Strolled back along the beach. A young woman getting a bit of sea air before going home to cook her husband's tea.'

Martin had an inch or so of beer left in his glass. He looked at his watch.

Sheepstone said, 'Oh, you're not in a hurry, Martin. You've got all the time in the world. Fancy another?'

'No, thanks.'

'Suit yourself. The briefcase was another little mistake, in my opinion. Oh, I understand why Annie got rid of it. A casually dressed young woman carrying a man's briefcase might have looked a bit odd. Attracted attention. You were hoping that anyone who saw her when she was disguised as Godley wouldn't remember it. But someone did. So you had to pretend that you'd forgotten all about it. You did it quite well, I must say. I was almost convinced.'

Martin lit a cigarette. He waved a wasp away and watched its flight.

'You took a gamble, of course, on Godley's clothes not being found until the following day. Someone walking his dog in the evening or a courting couple might have found them. But you'd worked out that it didn't really matter. You didn't report Godley's disappearance until nine twenty and you reckoned – correctly – that a Missing Person alert wouldn't be circulated until the following morning, at the earliest. So if anyone had found Godley's things on Wednesday evening and handed them in, the Exmouth coppers wouldn't have a clue who they belonged to. There was nothing in the pockets of Godley's coat that might have identified him, as you know. Are you sure you won't have another?'

'Yes. You're right. It does have a nasty aftertaste.'

'A short, then? Scotch? It might bring the colour back to your cheeks.'

'No. I'm all right.'

Sheepstone said, 'How did Annie get home, Martin? My best guess is she caught the five forty-five from Exmouth. It's busy at that time, what with folks who work in Exeter getting off, so the chances are nobody would pay her any particular attention. But I don't think she'd have taken a train all the way to Oke-hampton. Because there just might have been someone there who knew her. So I reckon she got off at Bel-stone Corner. There's no one manning that stop after five. You picked her up from there. Not in the Rolls, of course. In that old van that no one would look at twice. You drove her back to Burra Hall, then took the

Rolls to Okehampton to meet the last train at nine. A bit nip and tuck it would've been. But possible.'

Sheepstone paused, shook his head.

'By God, Martin, you must have been glad to see her. What an anxious day you'd had of it. Not knowing if she'd flunked it. Or buggered it up somehow. Bolsover said you were like a man with a teasel up his chuff. Which I'm sure you were. But not for the reasons he imagined. You didn't need to put on the bag of nerves act that day, did you?'

He waited. Wasps came, investigated, went away.

'Come on, Martin, say something. This is off the record. A chance meeting in a pub. No witnesses.'

Martin said, 'I had no idea that policemen had such vivid imaginations.'

'Of course we do,' Sheepstone said warmly. 'It's what we do. Take little bits and pieces, think about how they might join up, make them into a story with a beginning and a middle and an end. And then try to glue it to the truth. You need imagination to do that.'

'I suppose so, yes.'

'So,' Sheepstone said, 'you were a university man. Give my story marks out of ten. Eight? Eight and a half?'

'Two.'

'Strewth, that's harsh. Why so low?'

'Because whether we're talking about fact or fiction, you need a motive. Logic. I had no motive for murdering Mr Godley. Therefore your story doesn't work. At all.'

'You profited immensely from his death.'

'I had no idea that he'd left me anything.'

Sheepstone nodded. 'Reluctantly,' he said, 'I have to believe you. The copy of the will in Godley's bureau hadn't been tampered with. And if you'd nosed through his journal . . .'

'Which I hadn't.'

'. . . you'd have discovered that Godley'd had a, shall we say, difficult meeting with his solicitor back in February. But he doesn't give any details. So no, you didn't know that killing Godley would make you rich. Mind you, you were scared shitless when you found out. Never known sudden fortune make a man look so ill.'

Sheepstone smiled, relishing the memory. Then he sighed.

'But you're right, Martin. Two out of ten is generous, to be fair. Because good as it is, *true* as it is, my little story doesn't hang together because there's no logic to it. Why would two people conspire to murder a man who provided them with an income and a home?

One who treated them kindly? You'd have to believe they did it just because they wanted to. Because they could. Something as perverse as that.'

Sheepstone swilled back the last of his sour and now warm beer. He pulled a face.

'Do you believe in evil, Martin?'

'Yes.'

'Aye, of course you do. You'll have seen it in action. And you'll know it's infectious. Because you picked up a nasty dose of it somewhere. And you passed it on to Annie Luscombe. You corrupted her.'

'That happens to be pure nonsense.'

Sheepstone pulled the corners of his mouth down and cocked his head. 'Is it? I wonder what she would say if I were having this conversation with her rather than you.'

'She'd say nothing. She'd laugh. And in case you're thinking along those lines, I believe a wife can't be forced to give evidence against her husband.'

'Ah,' Sheepstone said and leaned back in his chair. 'When did this happy event take place?'

'Three weeks ago. Just a quiet do.'

'Yes, I imagine it would have been.' Sheepstone stood and put his hat on. 'If you believe in evil, Martin, does that mean you also believe in Hell?'

'Yes. I've been there.'

'Good. You'll know the way, then.'

After Sheepstone had gone, Martin sat on in the garden for a little while. He watched a wasp crawl down the inside of his almost empty glass. He placed a beer mat over the glass and waited until the insect became furiously aware of its predicament.

Then he folded his newspaper and went on his way.

2

IN EARLY SEPTEMBER his mother sent him a formal invitation to her wedding to Mr Neville Waters. Martin phoned her a couple of days later and offered to drive her to the church in the Rolls. To his surprise she accepted.

Peg prepared a hamper for the journey; as far as she was concerned, Dorchester was equidistant with Moscow. The Phantom, after a full day of Martin's attention, was eager.

'Where are we going, Martin?' Godley had asked him.

'Dorchester, sir. Then Blandford Forum.'

'Goodness, how exciting. The old girl hasn't been on a run like that since I bought her.'

As usual, Annie declined the luxury of the passenger compartment to sit beside Martin. She liked to be able to touch him frequently and she liked watching the Spirit of Ecstasy flying ahead of them, leading them on.

'Besides,' she said, putting her hands on the just-discernible swell of her belly, 'a few months from now, I'll not fit.'

Martin had been unable to entertain the notion of sleeping with Annie in his former, childhood, home. He was pretty sure that she would insist on mischievous – and noisy – sex in the guest bedroom adjacent to his mother's. So he'd booked them into the Royal Wessex. Annie had never stayed in a hotel before. Her girlish delight in the wickedness of it enchanted and aroused him.

Neville Waters drove Martin's mother to the Wessex for dinner. He was a tall man of about sixty and, Martin noted, considerably more handsome than his father had been. Clearly, he had looked forward to this first meeting with his future stepson with some trepidation; there was a slightly desperate edge to his geniality. Martin liked him.

Margery Heath was also a little ill at ease. She wanted it understood that she was not seeking her son's approval, but found herself needing it. She had told herself that it did not matter whether or not her fiancé approved of Martin, but found that it did. Towards her daughter-in-law she behaved with a kindly condescension to which Annie seemed blithely impervious; she had, to Martin's surprise and gratitude, decided to be demure for the evening. (On the quiet, she had arranged for a bottle of champagne, on ice, to be delivered to their room as soon as the desserts were served.)

Over the meal, the following day's arrangements were discussed. Martin would give his mother away. The Best Man was to be Neville's son, George. Here, Waters glanced anxiously at Martin.

'Good,' Martin said. 'Better him than me. I'm sure I'd flunk it.'

Over the brandy, the men talked about cars.

Annie perched her glass on the ledge beside the bath and scooped soapy water over her breasts.

'That went all right, I thought,' she said. 'I like your mum. Do you?'

Martin, seated on the toilet bowl, laughed. 'God, what a question. I don't know. She seems happy enough.'

'Of course she is. She's been getting fucked.'

'Annie!'

'What?'

'Has she?'

'Oh, yes. Definitely. I'd say they'd had a quick one earlier on.'

'Jesus. Really? How do you know?'

'I just do.' She reached for her glass and emptied it. 'More, please.'

He lifted the bottle from the bucket and, kneeling beside the bath, filled their glasses.

Annie said, 'Does it bother you? The idea of your mum having sex?'

'No.'

She lifted her left leg onto the rim of the bath and studied his face with ironic concern. 'Really? Not even when you imagine it? Her and Neville . . .'

He'd kept his hand in the ice bucket. Now, grinning, he plunged it into the bath, between her thighs. Annie squealed, holding her glass aloft and level.

He'd paid a young fellow from the Wessex ten bob to polish the Phantom. It waited, gleaming, outside his mother's house, as long as the front lawn was wide. Two pipe-smoking gentlemen had come to admire both it and Annie, who was tying bows of white ribbon to the mascot and the door handles.

Martin smoked a cigarette in the living room, waiting for his mother to come down. He noticed that certain items of furniture had disappeared. He stubbed the cigarette when he heard her footfall on the stairs.

'Well? Will I do, do you think?'

The suit was satin, the colour of a robin's egg. A little hat with a short lace veil that softened her eyes. Lipstick. Nylons and pale shoes with heels. He hardly knew her. He'd have passed her in the street. No, he'd have turned to admire her.

'Mutton dressed as lamb?'

'No, Ma. You look absolutely stunning. Honestly. Neville will fall over when he sees you.'

'Hmmn.' She went to the mirror and lifted the veil to re-examine her make-up. 'I'm selling the house,' she said, with her back to him.

'Of course. Why wouldn't you?'

'I thought you might want to take some of your old things away with you.'

He shrugged. 'I might. I'll think about it. Now then,

Mrs nearly Waters, it's time we went. Your carriage awaits.'

When he'd turned the Phantom onto the main road Martin looked up at the rear-view mirror. Harold Godley was studying his mother with frank admiration. The old boy met Martin's reflected eyes and rolled his own with comedic lasciviousness. Martin laughed aloud then returned his gaze to the road and to Ecstasy, trailing wedding ribbon, leaning into the hurtling air.

Editorial Note

This novel is a masterpiece and something of an enigma. Is it a ghost story? Is it a murder story? Is it something else entirely? It is also quintessentially British. I have now read it a number of times and each time I read it I like it more. It was, I think, the very last book Mal Peet wrote. He lived to complete it, but not to see it published, nor did he live to revise and edit. On the principle of 'Here the maestro put down his pen' I have decided to leave his words just as he wrote them, no more no less.

However, Mal did leave himself one or two very

puzzling author notes which were marked in capitals in the typescript. These have been incorporated in 'the naming of the parts'. Again these are all Mal's own words.

It may be a coincidence that the hero of this story is a British squaddie returning damaged from the last war for European unity, but I can't help feeling that this novel resonates very loudly in the world right now. Its relevance seems to ring out in every daily news bulletin I watch or hear. The phrase 'An infection of evil' is important because it describes how not all evil is intentional. Part three is the key I feel . . . the crime . . . the murder . . . ? 'YOU FIT MY WOUNDS EXACTLY' was Mal's note to himself right there in the script. But whose wounds did he mean?

David Fickling
11ᵗʰ November 2017
Remembrance Day

Mal Peet and
Mr Godley's Phantom:
A Ghost Story

I have no idea whether Mal Peet believed in ghosts. I don't believe in them myself, and yet this book is a ghost story, perhaps several, and I believe every word. It is many kinds of book rolled into one: a story about a man recovering from trauma, a historical novel, and even a police procedural. But, yes, I think it's mostly a ghost story, and my favourite kind.

We don't meet any real ghosts till the latter part of this book, but it's been a ghost story all along. It's about two men, both alive (just about), both haunted by their losses and their traumas from the two World Wars. Those, then are its ghosts – those persistent haunting presences in the lives of the living, the unforgiving, devastating things that are alive and real in our memory. Not the ghosts we see with our eyes, floating around implausibly under bedsheets clanking chains and going *WHOOOO!!!* – but the ones which come to us whether we're waking or sleeping, unsummoned, into our mind's eye.

Several of Mal's books are, like this one, troubled by the way people drag the past along with them, and by how that affects their lives today. How to deal with that pain? How to carry on? The books often span generations, and take an interest in what happened *then*, but mostly in order to ask: how did that lead us to *now*? Historical settings reveal something about today. So *Life: An Exploded Diagram* is, yes, a coming-of-age story about a Norfolk lad, but it's also (though we might not know it) the story of the older man looking back, to what made him – the man that Norfolk lad became. *Mr Godley's Phantom* is not about war itself, but about people for whom almost intolerable post-war grief has become the default state – every bit of fight they have left is spent just keeping it merely bearable.

Before reading this final Mal Peet novel, I treated myself – and it was such a treat – to rereading the seven that came before it, almost-but-not-quite in order. Eight books in total, which make up The Complete Novels of Mal Peet. The experience was bittersweet, of course, a pang of sadness and of indignation that such a thing as The Complete Novels of Mal Peet already exists! (How can this be all we're getting? Surely we were promised more?) But there was also great pleasure in seeing the work together, composing the picture of what it adds up to.

Well, then. My story – another ghost story of sorts – begins fifteen years ago, with the appearance of Mal's first 'Young Adult' novel. (I won't go into what that means, as I can't think of a writer for whom the categorisation is more irrelevant.) *Keeper* introduced us to a terrific central character and his world. (Mal would return to both three years later in *Penalty* – his most underrated book, to my mind.) *Keeper* won the Branford Boase Award, a 'best debut' prize with an impressive track record not only in rewarding talent, but spotting promise of more to come.

Those prize judges were right – what a start it was. Not every writer who produces a great first novel can then keep it up. Some find they only really have one or two good books in them, they've said all they have to say and everything that follows is bit of a disappointment; some get rushed, under pressure to produce something for a waiting readership and impatient publishers (*Keeper* came seemingly from nowhere, it had no readers awaiting it); some just get lazy. But Mal started great, and got better.

I attended a 'Children's Writers' Question Time' event at the Hay Festival many years ago where a lad in the audience asked the panel anxiously, 'What advice would you give a reader about choosing their next book, when they're convinced that the *last* thing they read was the best book in the whole world and nothing else will ever match up?' One of the panellists – I think it was Patrick Ness – asked the boy, out of interest, what he'd just read that had brought this crisis on? It was a book called *Exposure*, he said, a book by Mal Peet. (I later pointed out to Mal that he had basically managed single-handedly to destroy reading forever for this poor kid.)

Mal would follow *Exposure*, this apparently unimprovable book, with something better. *Life: An Exploded Diagram* comes as close to a perfect contemporary novel as any I know. Everyone, simply, should read it. It has all the qualities of, well, almost everything Mal wrote, but not least the ability, by some baffling sleight of hand, to make small things, on the scale of unassuming individual lives, seem like the most important thing in the world. Though Mal could do the big picture, too, of course, when he wanted – and (harder still) was a deft handler of the simultaneity of the two. There's one paragraph in *Life* that starts with a boatful of revolutionaries leaving Mexico for Cuba (Che Guevara, Fidel Castro and co.), and by the time the paragraph ends some dozen lines later we're in a Norfolk lane with an unfortunate lad who's just had his cap chucked on the back of a passing lorry by the local bully. The switching between the two is a subtle effect, highly ambitious . . . and yet sort of typical.

I don't know whether Mal thought of himself as a brave or ambitious writer – he may have had no truck with such praise – but he certainly seemed so to me. His Carnegie Medal winner *Tamar* is set across three time periods – there's a 1945, and a 1995, and an implied 'now' – but it's structurally braver than even that suggests. (It's also very occasionally funny, when he notices things and can't help himself.)

Tamar, another war novel of sorts, is about the stories we choose to keep secret, to keep private, and what happens when we tell them. And *Exposure* itself is in part about celebrity . . . Now I think about it, there's a lot in Mal's work about how we choose to show ourselves to the outside world – it's in this very book you've just finished reading, isn't it? Remember those early exchanges between Martin and Annie, where he is aware of the fake jollity of his speech? It's in the conversations that very deliberately aren't had ('the honest words hung silent in the air between them'), in the woman who 'seethed with questions she didn't know how to ask', in the choices made not to reveal the truth about ourselves if we can help it. Annie 'had two ways of speaking, two voices. One her own, one borrowed.' We do see tiny revelations of the vulnerable inner self all the time, but they're inadvertent. They're all so well-observed, these tiny things that we readers can't help believe because this is how people truly are. Mal may have been a writer of fiction, but in eight novels I don't think I ever once caught him lying.

Our author is himself careful what he does and doesn't reveal to us, too. In *Tamar* he seems wilfully to defuse a great emotional moment by pre-announcing an important death hundreds of pages before it happens; and at one point *Mr Godley* becomes something like a murder mystery – except that Mal, uninterested in the old narrative conventions, blithely solves the murder for us around the halfway mark. Meanwhile other significant things are more surprisingly withheld, so we readers aren't even allowed to make our minds up about what the title is referring to (the ghost haunting Mr Godley? the Rolls-Royce? the ghost *of* Mr Godley?), as he changes our minds for us again and again, layer added to layer. Even that three-word title works hard.

Mal Peet produced some of the least *lazy* writing I've ever read. He manages so much in so few incredibly economical lines. Look at how much he gets done in just this book's first couple of paragraphs. (His opening sequence to *Life: An Exploded Diagram* is, incidentally, possibly the best piece of condensed narrative I have ever read.) Or look at page sixteen, where he manages to make you feel deep and painful sympathy for a character you literally only met a dozen lines earlier!

And he chooses words with such care. They're never approximate, never just-good-enough, always exactly right. He's a great coiner of language, but a subtle one, and he makes individual words do things you didn't know they could. (Flicking through my copy of *Tamar*, I see I underlined the word 'surly' on page 87. It is used to describe a sofa. It is – implausibly – the perfect word.)

I've only seen a couple of his pre-edited manuscripts, and while I've invariably had editorial thoughts, they're always about how things might change only on a big structural scale; but taking it line by line and word by word it always looks perfect. He talked openly about the difficulties he encountered in writing, how hard it was to get a book right, how hard it was just to get the damn thing *done*. But reading him you'd never know it.

Not that he tried to make life easy for himself. Think of *The Murdstone Trilogy*, the last book published in his lifetime, utterly different from anything he'd ever done before. 'A bit of a leap in the dark, this one,' he said. (It's the only one where his wicked humour is allowed off the leash entirely, and it's such fun to watch.) Or of the uncompromising, psychologically complex book which eventually – with Meg Rosoff's collaboration – became the posthumous *Beck*. Another book about dealing with hardship, but more importantly about becoming. About the character becoming who he became.

Every novel of Mal's improves with re-reading – that's certainly true for *Mr Godley's Phantom*. It's a good posterity test for a book, I think. Mal gives us more with each re-encounter; and in his best books, he gives us wonders of character and prose on every page.

He *gives* us?

Yes, that's the prerogative of a great artist – as long as we read him, he can be forever in the present tense.

We're told quite firmly, as students of literature, that we must resist assuming too much about writers themselves from their books. We learn that this blurring is unhelpful, and naïve. But how are we to believe someone could write books so humming with warmth and wit, generosity and mischief, insight and compassion, if the writer wasn't such a person? Mal was, I think; and thanks to these books, he still is. And that's the very best kind of ghost story, the most generous and the most benign kind of sustaining afterlife I can imagine. The book you're holding in your hands is a part of that.

The End.

But . . . not really.

Daniel Hahn
Reader, fan and friend of Mal Peet

Acknowledgements

To John Schofield and John Field, for introducing Mal to one of the main characters of Mr Godley's Phantom.

Thanks to John Schofield for allowing us to spend time looking at, and reclining in, his Rolls-Royce Phantom III, H J Mulliner Sedanca de Ville.

Thanks to John Field for showing us his beautiful collection of Rolls-Royces – and for the free-range duck eggs.

To the IIML at Victoria University in Wellington, New Zealand, for providing Mal with space and time to write *Mr Godley's Phantom*. Special thanks to Bill

Manhire for the invitation, and to Damien Wilkins for the hospitality. And thanks to everyone else in Wellington whose warmth and welcome made the time that Mal spent writing *Mr Godley's Phantom* such fun.

Elspeth Graham-Peet